NELSC

If one studies the Weismantel family tree back to the year 1500, there is one common denominator that is easily recognized, namely fathers insisted on naming their sons after themselves. This shows up time and time again with the names John, Bernardo, Guy, Gregory, Matthew, Robert, Michael, Nicholas, Mark and Charles cropping up many times, along with modifications and nicknames out of these same roots.

It is no wonder that in the years leading to 2084, that there were three generations of the "Charles" root starting with Charles, then Charlie Junior (also called CJ) and finally, Chuck. And, like in many families, the sons followed in their father's occupational footsteps. BUT –

The original Weismantels were tailors. In fact, the original surname was Schneider, which, in German is translated as tailor. But, back in 1500, Hans Schneider wore a white cloak as he traveled about The Village of Bad Kissingen, and the populous gave him the

i

nickname, "Hans White Cloak," and that is how the name Weismantel began.

In Germany, the 's' is really an ettsett, (that sounds like two ss'es. Ettsett appears after Z in the German alphabet) however in the U.S. the ettsett letter was reduced to one simple single 's'. From 1500 until the early 1900s, the tradition of Weismantels being tailors was found throughout Europe, and, the same held true in the United States, where tailors with this name were found in the Midwest in Waukegan, Illinois, St. Charles, Illinois, and Lancaster, Ohio. And, in the Southwest, at least one of these tailors migrated to Houston, namely, *Barney the Tailor.*

Barney the Tailor was well known for his clothing made for leaders and members of the Big Bands during that era of time. From band uniforms, Barney switched to making military uniforms for pilots graduating with their wings from Ellington Field. That airbase is just South of Houston, Texas. He also had a store in Hondo, Texas that served navigators during the Second World War.

Barney's clothes were stylish and they often appeared in Esquire in the years when Esquire was the magazine known for the beautiful woman in the foldout centerfold of each issue. Everyone knew when a person was wearing a *Barney the Tailor* suit because the pocket was on the right hand side of the coat instead of, normally for men, on the left. And—Barney's suit and sport coats always had four open buttons on the sleeves—and—the Barney style was to wear only two of them closed—the two closest to the elbow—and the two closest to the hand always remained unbuttoned. Barney's clothes were well-known, world-wide.

Barney presented each suit to the wearer with a hand-painted Countess Mara tie. She (the Countess) was still alive in the 1940s and Barney often flew to New York to visit her in person to pick out ties for his own clients. The countess always scrolled her initials at the bottom of each tie that she hand-painted by using an ornate italic CM that looked just like a CW. She never revealed the kind of paint that she used for these very expensive silk ties..........and..........while everyone graciously called her countess, Barney never knew her last name, or where she came from, or if she were true royalty.

The Countess' two biggest fans were Barney....and....Frank Sinatra, who felt that wearing a CM was the essence of being a gentleman. Barney, if he were alive today, could simply turn to Wikipedia to learn all about Countess Lucille Mara de Vescovi, daughter of an Italian baroness and grand-daughter of a European Countessa, both of whom were legends in sartorial dressing.

In the mid-1950s, for the Weismantels, chemical engineering replaced tailoring as the family's key profession. And, from then until 2084, three generations of Chem E's followed in succession. And—true to form—this succession passed the root name of Charles from one generation to the next. In birth order, Charles, Charlie Junior (CJ), and Chuck --were all chemical engineers. In fact, Charles' wife, Cathy, also had that profession...a profession that was and is still closely watched by the U.S. government after the tragedy of 9-11.

Government officials, especially the watchdogs for terror, know that chemists and chemical engineers have the brains and capability of producing weapons of mass destruction. Under The Patriot Act, the government monitors even the students who are taking chemical engineering, just as closely as they monitor anyone taking flying lessons.

Chemical engineers form the basis of the nuclear industry, the biotech industry and the explosives industries. E.I. duPont deNemours & Company made its fortune manufacturing black powder during the civil war and that explosives industry, based on nitrogen chemistry, particularly nitrocellulose and tri-nitro-toluene, TNT, is still the basis of military incendiaries and explosives...especially large explosives.

With this background, it is no wonder that three generations of Weismantels, carrying over three generations of chemical engineers who understand basic nitrogen chemistry, find themselves as watchees by watchers working for Big Brother, a name used to describe the federal government way back when—when there was a book titled: 1984.

By 2084, however, as you will read, a much more dangerous force exists in the United States.........it is a threat tied to an extrapolation of what took place in 1984. It, the force, started in 2003 or a bit before, when a seed was planted by Congress that grew into a belief allowing presidents to believe they can act as king.......a facet of the presidency that the public has not been able to rein in due to people, power and dollars of $F = ma$.

CHARLES	CATHY	CJ	ALVETA	CHUCK
Charles Born 1936				
Graduated UT 1958 @ age 22	Cathy Born 1958 (Charles is 22)			
Charles + Cathy Marriage 1980 (Charles is 44) (Cathy is 22) 1981 – Thomas 1983 – Brenda 1986 – George 1989 – Fredrick 1991 – Arthur 1992 – Edward 1996 – Charlie Junior		Charlie Junior (CJ) Born 1996 (Charles is 60) (Cathy is 38)	Alveta Born 2010	
Charles dies 2022 @ age 86 (CJ is 26)	Cathy dies 2018 @ age 60 (CJ is 22)	CJ Graduates UT 2017		
		CJ + Alveta Marriage 2032 (CJ is 36) (Alveta is 22) 2036 – Alley 2040 – Katherine 2042 – Chuck		Chuck Born 2042
			Alveta dies 2046 @ age 36 (Chuck is 4, CJ is 50)	Chuck Graduates UT 2062
		In 2084...	CJ is 88 Widowed	Chuck is 42 Single

Chuck, born in 2042, never knew his grandparents
Charlie Junior's siblings and Chuck's siblings also shown

Nelson Gregory's 2084: COPYRIGHT 2008

Preface
A Note from the Publisher

2084 is not your normal book. Its presentation begins with three chapters that introduce the main characters. Charles & Cathy (Chapter One in the year 2003), Charlie Junior (CJ) and Alveta (Chapter Two in the year 2032) and Chuck (Chapter Three in the year 2084). These chapters hint at the central story, which is how three generations of The Weismantel Family (and a group of peers) recognize that the U.S. government is changing—changing to become a dictatorship. And—there is a powerful group of individuals and organizations that intend to control and dominate. We have included a "chart of years" in the INTRODUCTION to assist the reader.

Chapters Four through Twenty-Three (Note the year associated with each chapter) relate a series of events, not in chronological order, that describe some of the complications that are taking place, politically, in the USA that began at the turn of the century and were exacerbated into an attack on civil liberties, personal freedom and the rights of the individual. The problems associated with this evolution is first recognized by Charles & Cathy, who, pass down—through Charlie Junior & Alveta and eventually to Chuck—that their family must do something to assure that citizens are not overpowered by the federal government with an encroachment on freedom. These central chapters hint at the Weismantel plan over the decades....and....how the goals and objectives are transferred between generations through the company they own: White Cloak LLC.

Chapters Twenty-Four through Thirty use the titles of Winston Churchill's series of books that warn of, and deal with, the impending and actual threats of a ruthless dictator who had no compunctions of using annihilation of certain citizens to meet his terrible objectives. These chapters suggest a parallel set of events is taking place in the United States.

Then—the last two chapters of the book—create the most tragic Valentine's Day massacre that one could ever imagine as U.S. troops, backed by Blackwater-Xe mercenaries, attack U.S. citizens on our own soil. The plan to protect ourselves against the government (that has been breeding through three generations of Weismantels) must be put into action.

Nelson Gregory is the pseudonym of a 72-year-old Republican that believes the GOP is no longer following the basic principles of why he joined the party in 1958 after graduating college with a Bachelor of Science in Chemical Engineering. He suggests that being a true Republican means supporting:

- A balanced budget
- Moving decision making to the lowest level of government
- Rights of the individual.....to include supporting the Bill of Rights
- Congress must declare war—not leave the decision-making to the president
- Establishing rules for business that insist on integrity and fairness
- Free enterprise (that does not bail out investment houses that make bad decisions)
- Legislation without earmarks

- <u>Balance of payments of exports and imports must be in line</u>
- <u>The family is the most important level of decision making.</u>
- <u>Video monitoring by the government within a person's home is an invasion of privacy.</u>

Nelson Gregory has published hundreds of articles and several books (technical and business). He has worked in the paint business, for McGraw-Hill and now has a private consulting practice.

Reviewers Comments:

*   Powerful observation by an everyday Republican of what will happen when Americans give too much power to a president.

* England did not heed Churchill's warnings of Hitler. Will the U.S. heed Nelson Gregory's warning of the enemy within? *2084* uses, as chapter titles, the series of Churchill's books, except Nelson Gregory changes Their Finest Hour to Their Saddest Hour. Churchill ends his speech with the words: "Let us brace ourselves..." Apparently that is exactly what the author is asking the American people to do...."Brace yourself because we have met the enemy and they are us."

* Orwell's 1984 may have been a test of reality. Nelson Gregory's *2084* will become reality if voters in the USA elect a Congress that gives rubber-stamp approvals to a regal-like president.

* It is a scary thought that the people of the United States will be attacked by Blackwater-Xe

mercenaries hired to protect our borders......this is not a job where you hire a corporation.

* I hope that readers understand that the Detroit Muslims represent the same things as Jews in Germany, Irish Catholics, Blacks, WASPS and Hispanics....and...one-hundred other groups. Anyone can get finger-pointed by federal authorities (sometimes without warrant).

* The idea behind *2084* seems quite simple. Only Congress has the constitutional right to declare war. Giving that permission-to-go-to-war to the president is an abrogation of Congressional responsibility. Where is the Supreme Court when you need them to enforce the system of checks and balances? We need to elect a Congress with b a _ _ s.

* Government in-your-face started with the cameras at the traffic light and it has extended to monitoring your phone calls without warrant or oversight by the judicial system. Nelson Gregory is pleading with the voters to reverse

the trend of usurped power by the president and agencies.

* Congress keeps passing legislation (even today with the Democrats in charge of both houses) that allows the president to rule as king. When the USA Secretary of Defense and the Attorney General approve torture, the government is out of control.

* Too much government is too much government even if there is a threat of terror in the world.

* At Del Mar, California, government regulations prevent you from enjoying a glass of wine on the beach as you quietly watch the sunset over the ocean. Did POGO have it right? Maybe it should have been "We have met the money and they have us." Will Blackwater-Xe guard the beach?

* *2084* has just enough love and boy-girl stuff to make this thriller worth reading again and again. It is time to vote-away entrenched politicians. They have entirely too much control.

* I'm hooked!! BUT--What is Chuck going to do in 2085?

* I want to sample the "heavy, hearty, Hungarian sauces" and the stuffed cabbage.

* I love the alliteration....and...2π radians is still 360 degrees no matter how you look at it.

TABLE OF CONTENTS

CHAPTER ONE
2003 – CHARLES & CATHY

There was an **antique mirror** hanging over the fireplace ..... and ..... their house had two very large picture windows overlooking one of the largest back yards in Kingwood. Charles looked at Cathy as she reached and leaned forward over the back of a long leather couch and turned the rod that opened the louvers of the vertical Venetian blinds covering those windows opening the view to that yard. As she did so, the suns rays crept down and landed directly on her right ankle and highlighted the woman's shapely calf. Her heel was about four inches in the air, toes bent, as she stretched to perform the louver duty. Charles' eyes riveted on his wife's beauty, from her knee to her toe. Twenty-two years her senior, he never stopped appreciating Cathy's beauty. Neither seven childbirths, nor the workload she had shouldered throughout their entire marriage, had taken one iota from her girlish figure – and – at 45 she still looked as chase as she did at 22 on their wedding day wearing a size 6 dress.

"Would you do that again," he said, aloud. She was still leaning, and glanced over her right shoulder and replied: "Do what?" Charles smiled: "Lift your heel about four inches off the ground so I can look at your leg." Cathy giggled flirtatiously, and did what he asked her to do in a coy, innocently seductive move that brought happiness to both husband and wife. With the sunbeams following her, she jumped down from the couch and hopped four steps to where he stood and landed in his arms.

They embraced, simply looking at each other—with eyes mesmerized—his blues magnetized to hers of ochre. Neither had to say a word. With a million megahertz, they hugged one another, locked together. Had anyone walked into the room they would feel the force that was bonding these lovers. Yet, there was no kiss, no passion – simply total knowledge of each other's thoughts for that single moment – a moment that had carried through two decades of empathy.

"Always!" he said. That is the single word he used time and time again. He did not have to say three little words. He said those three often enough in deeds, but the word "always" meant more – much, much more.

"Infinity to the infinity power?" she replied in a question. And with that question their heads threw back, and both mouths open widely in hilarious laughter. <u>Nothing</u> was greater than "infinity to the infinity power," an expression that their children, especially Charlie Junior, used to indicate he was the best, or had the most of anything. Today Cathy used it to weigh the value of their love.

Charles sat down in the big blue chair...the one he had bought for Cathy several years ago so that she could curl up within its three large pillows to stay warm and feel the softness that came from pure down. She actually used that chair when Charles was traveling.

Today she curled up in the corner of the sofa, reached up and turned on the table lamp and began to read the paper with an exclamation in reaction to a major headline: "Did you see the President signed a $3 billion nano-technology bill yesterday?"

Charles, as a chemical engineer, was deeply involved with paints and coatings and fine-particulate filtration. He had followed the nano-legislation carefully because he felt certain this would benefit his consulting practice. "Not only did I see it," he said, "but Nugent and I spent an hour on the phone discussing the bill's approval."

He paused.

He continued.

"After Nuge and I talked, I called Congressman Poe to get a copy of the final draft, and I'm trying to find out who lobbied for it. There is some big money involved and it is important for us to understand who Bush will be rewarding. We may have to join that band wagon."

When Charles said "us" he meant more than him and Dr. Nugent Neulone. He meant to include Cathy in particular because being a chemical engineer herself, she was intently involved in every project Charles did. She knew how to write and put together reports better than himself.

The quiet moment followed by serious conversation turned into turmoil a moment later as their seven-year-old son, Charlie Junior, bounced into the room, arms outstretched, zooming like an airplane and with all the roaring sounds to match. The seven-year-old growled jet airplane noises from his throat.

Cathy looked at him and said: "Airplanes fly outside CJ!", and immediately Charlie Junior was out the door.

CHAPTER TWO
2032 – CHARLIE JUNIOR (CJ) & ALVETA

Charlie Junior knew that the Fields family had owned Rosewood Cemetery for over a century. Jack Fields had been Congressman for the area in the 1990s and Jack often told the story of how he had to go door-to-door selling cemetery plots when he was only fourteen. "That must have been a hard sell," CJ said to himself.

He made his way down the dirt path of the cemetery to a location just beyond the fruitless pear tree, and there, in front of him, was the simple stone of the Weismantel Family plot.

It read:

==========================

Cathy Weismantel   1958 – 2018

A most loving mother and wife who spent her whole life giving

Charles Weismantel   1936 – 2022

Time with the one you love is the most precious thing on earth

==========================

It was hard to believe that his dad, twenty-two years older than his mom, had outlived her by four years.

He stood beside the graves and said out loud: "I wish you both were going to be here." Tomorrow, he and Alveta would be married at St. Mary's Catholic Church in Humble. Retired Monsignor Paul would administer the sacrament at 10:10 AM That time was chosen in memory of CJ's dad who always made appointments at 10:10, 11:11, 2:02, 3:03 or 3:33........the idea being that neither he nor his client would forget the time.

Charlie Junior prayed silently, saying the joyful mysteries of the Rosary. During his recollection of The Visitation, he remembered his cousin Elizabeth. He always remembered her during this decade because Mary went to visit her own cousin, Elizabeth, after learning from Angel Gabriel that both she and Elizabeth would conceive.

CJ prayed openly, asking for graces of a happy marriage for him and Alveta. She was fourteen years younger than he. "I'm just like dad," he laughed to himself thinking how strange it was to realize that—when he was

7

graduating with his Bachelor of Science in Chemical Engineering—Alveta was just finishing the second grade. Years later, after Alveta had graduated from Stanford, she adopted the UT "Hook 'em Horns" attitude and attended many reunions honoring the legendary people whose names adorn the Engineering Buildings at the corner of Speedway and Dean Bolton Blvd.

CJ's dad had loved UT even though his BS ChE was from the University of Notre Dame in South Bend, Indiana. When asked about his loyalties, his dad would say: "I love them both."

CJ finished his rosary and headed to Will Clayton Blvd and IAH where he was to pick up Alveta, who was returning from California. She had joined Dream Works after graduation, and because her major was in computer graphics and animation, she was the ideal person to be part of the company's newly opened Houston office. Her expertise was widely sought after because so much animation is generated by computer. Her matriculation at Stanford had led to a summer work program at Dream Works – at the corporate headquarters in California— and—being from Texas had made her move to

Texas geographically synergistic for both company and employee.

As for Charlie Junior (people who knew him well often called him CJ), prior to taking over the family business, He had been with a spin-off of duPont for a short time where he specialized in the manufacture of nitrocellulose and acrylic lacquers – the former still widely used in new housing construction, and the latter for automobiles. Ironically, Toyota's new VIOS plant in the U.S., which would build the car that that company first introduced in China, would be using an acrylic paint formulated by CJ himself when he was with duPont. This move to a U.S. supplier was a breakthrough in dismantling the Shiatsu that for many years had been integral to most Japanese purchases here in the United States.

CHAPTER THREE
2084 – CHUCK

Chuck genuflected and made the sign of the cross as he entered the second pew from the front of Saint Martha, Mary and Lazarus, Friends of Jesus, Catholic Church in Kingwood, Texas. It was a very old church from the previous century (the new one being built in 2010) in need of painting. He was early for 7:30 AM Sunday morning mass when he arrived forty-five minutes before the priest. Yet, when he walked in, there was already a young man standing idly in the vestibule. He was probably the government's monitor.

Federal monitors always looked the same, just like California Highway Patrolmen wear mustaches; they (monitors) were all cast from the same mold. This man met the stereotype requirements by wearing a dark blue suit, nothing obtuse, a standard less-than-Brooks-Brothers suit, no Windsor knot in the tie, and every piece of clothing positioned to blend in with its surroundings as if he wasn't there at all. But he – or she in some cases – was <u>always</u> there.

Indeed – always there – even though there was no law to prevent church gatherings. While government permits were required if more then fifty people were to be at any location, churches were permit-exempt. This number fifty, however, gave the DTC (Department of Terrorism Control – formerly the Department of Homeland Security) the right to send a representative, a monitor, to any gathering of such size...even churches. It was in fact not unusual for DTC to send someone to a family reunion...especially a family reunion...because the feeling or government's consensus thinking was that family members tend to think alike and offer the opportunity for covert planning against the government.

Everyone knew that DTC reps were always present at mass, at temple and all major congregational services. It was common knowledge that when any religious establishment or non-profit organization applied for its 501c3 status from the Internal Revenue Service, the IRS automatically informed DTC. The latter, openly, and without embarrassment, often put a member of the congregation on the DTC payroll to provide weekly reports of church activity to include names of parishioners, committee chairpersons and board members. This information went into a federal data bank that the man on the street referred to as GEORGE, Government Eyes on Organizations Everywhere. Some added the world "curious" because, indeed, it was that.

As Chuck kneeled to say the five mysteries of the rosary related to the Life of Christ, he ignored the other occupant in the rear of the church. Chuck's mind rattled off the first mystery: The Wedding Feast at Cana – and – off he went praying one Our Father and ten Hail Marys.

These 15 minutes of silent prayer before mass were sacred to Chuck, especially in the quiet darkness of the morn. With anticipation he looked forward to these 900 seconds because this time of prayer was such a soothing massage to the brain. It took his mind off matters of a police state. Prayer, in some ways, was just like skiing or fishing.

When one skis, all thoughts, all worries, all memories are shed from the brain as if they didn't exist. The only thing that you think about is the mogul directly in front of you, and the anticipation of the next one. As the skis slam into the mogul, in a turning motion, the athlete twists and side-slips down the face of the hump – and – time and time again turns are repeated in a muscular melody of highs and lows that manually moves a person down the hill with the exhilaration of a rhapsody or the thunder of the War of 1812 Overture.

Fishing creates a similar mesmerized mentality.

Chuck began the second mystery of the rosary by whispering to himself: <u>The Baptism of Jesus by his Cousin, John</u>. Then he prayed an Our Father and Ave, Ave, Ave, Ave, Ave, Ave, Ave, Ave, Ave, Ave + Glory be to the Father and to the Son and the Holy Spirit, as it was in the beginning, is now, and ever shall be, world without end, Amen...Now he went on to the third mystery...<u>The Transfiguration</u>...

For a brief moment, Chuck's mind wondered away from the beads as the church doors opened and parishioners, particularly older parishioners, so common at early masses, began to arrive. Older people always frequented the 7:30 AM mass. While not that old, Chuck often considered it a game to guess people's ages. He never knew if he was right or wrong, but, at 42 years old, he was often mistaken for 34, and, similarly, his dad, who was still called Charlie Junior, did not look or act like 88.

His dad's mind was still as sharp as a tack; his dad had just learned that a fourth patent application had been accepted on a unique Gravitation Energy Device, the GED, which is a way to turn the earth's gravity into electrical power.

Chuck's thoughts turned to the fourth mystery – The Beatitudes. Chuck prayed more quickly and reached the Institution of the Blessed Sacrament.......the fifth and final mystery.

There…in a wisp, he had completed all the beads.

Once the rosary was done, Chuck sat down in the pew and used his right foot to lift the kneeler, storing it under the seat in front of him. He did this just as a young woman entered that front pew. He quickly returned the kneeler to the down position so that when she knelt, her feet would not hit the kneeler – which would have happened had he left it up.

Why the concern? Because the woman was tall and thin, long-legged body, with shapely ankles – and she wore long, black pointed-toe shoes that perfectly matched her black stretch-knit slacks, black sweater, and black leather jacket.

Ladies in black always caught Chuck's bachelor blue eyes. As he returned the kneeler to the floor, the woman, probably in her mid-to-late twenties, not wearing a wedding ring – used her left hand to straighten the rear of her pants. They didn't need straightening but she performed the duty twice moving her hand from waist to hip to thigh across a firm derriere that had not gone unnoticed by a man who was no longer thinking about any one of the mysteries of the rosary.

"Having this princess in front of me for forty-five minutes is just not going to work," Chuck said to himself. But, there she was – directly in front of him – through the priest's procession in, the homily, the offertory, the consecration and the communion – and the procession out. Chuck let her leave first so that he could follow her out whichever door she chose to leave.

And…no sooner did they clear the door when he tapped the woman on her shoulder.

"Miss," he said. And then he stopped mid-sentence!

{Do you ever have your mind race?}

{The brain thinks a thousand times faster than one can speak.}

Chuck had said "Miss" but in the moment of silence before the next word was uttered, his mind asked:

Am I really doing this?

Why am I doing this?

Is this really me talking?

And – as quickly as he had asked himself each question, he answered, "Yes" to all three of his mental questions, and in an instant added: There's still time to change the subject……. But he did not change.

He continued: "Miss, my name is Chuck Weismantel; I was seated directly behind you all during mass." Chuck knew she had seen him because after the Our Father, she turned to him to offer a sign of peace and she shook his hand. Her hand was strong yet soft – like a woman who enjoyed gardening with her gloves on. She did not wear a wedding ring.

He continued to embarrass himself saying: "I just wanted you to know that I have to go to another mass this morning, because I could not concentrate on anything that was being said by the priest at this one." He stammered a bit, adding: "Please excuse me for being so blunt, but you are so attractive that I just couldn't pay attention in church and was anxious for mass to end so I could introduce myself," and he handed her his business card. "Someday," he said, "I would certainly like to have a tête-à-tête over a cup of coffee."

Just as quickly as the last word came out of his mouth, he expected to experience a crash landing, but – perhaps because he had used the word tête-à-tête, she replied: "Parlez-vous France?"

His jaw dropped almost to his waist. The French reply came totally unexpected, and he was pleased that he had not heard the words "Laissez-moi tranquille," a French form of "get lost." In his own cryptic French with a switch into English he responded: "Je comprends, but, only enough to get myself in trouble."

They both laughed, and then she replied in English: "Do you always attend 7:30 AM mass?"

"Only when I can't sleep," he joked, and said: "Do you?"

She thought for a moment, then in a suggestive mode said: "I'm really an eleven o'clock mass kind of girl," and smiled. "Maybe we can have a donut in the Family Life Center some Sunday after mass."

"May I call you to confirm?" Chuck responded without hesitation, and before he could say Jack Robinson, she said: "I'm Gloria Switzer," and she had whipped a pen from her purse, writing her phone number on the back of his card, and with a smile placed her order: "Please give me a call, Chuck....what was your last name again?"

"Weismantel" he said, emphasizing the three syllables. "It means white cloak in German. Weis is white and mantel is cloak."

She lifted her eyes as if to think, and then added: "Indeed it does." This told Chuck that maybe she also spoke German, but just as he was about to ask, the monitor approached them. Not wanting to create any more suspicion than he had already done by passing a card back and forth, he tenderly took her elbow and said: "May I walk you to your car?" And she said, "Sure." They left the monitor standing where they had just stood.

CHAPTER FOUR
2004 – THE ICEBERG SPEECH

Little Charlie Junior entered the family room and pounced down on the couch next to his mom. Cathy was intent, watching President Bush on TV as her husband sat in the big blue, extra-comfy chair that he had bought especially for her. Charles – also intent – did not even notice that Charlie Junior was nestling into his mother's armpit. The only voice was that of the president.

But, every now and then, Charles would bellow out a criticism in reaction to the president's speech. Charles, a conservative Republican, was certainly not agreeing with Bush even though he had voted for him. He did not intend to ever vote for him again. Charles called Bush a liar, a charlatan, and a spend-a-holic.

At 60 years old, Charles had been highly critical of AARP's backing of the changes in Medicare that effectively gave drug companies the right to rip-off the elderly. During that part of the president's speech, he muttered one word: "Unbelievable."

Charles, like Cathy, also believed that the Bush war on terrorism was leading to untold loss of freedom, and, individual's rights were being obliterated in the name of security. Bush was growing government in quantum leaps, and both the national debt and the balance of payments problem was asymptotic. When Bush said his tax cuts were working to improve the economy, Charles blurted out: "at the expense of my children and their grandchildren."

Bush bragged about successes in Afghanistan and Charles reacted by saying: "the warlords and dopers have more control than ever and women still have no rights." The massacre of hundreds by the war lord, Abdul Rojan, was not mentioned.

Bush bragged about Iraqi freedom and Charles said: "We are going to turn the country over to the Shiites and Iran because he (meaning Bush) didn't have one strategic plan in mind before invading."

Bush bragged about success in Libya and North Korea and Charles just laughed out loud.

When Bush talked about more federal involvement in schools, Charles replied satirically: "Boy, that's just what we need. More taxes so that DC bureaucrats can dole out money to their favorite voting blocks."

When Bush talked about his forward strategy of freedom, Charles looked at Cathy and said, bluntly: "What that means is more war."

One after the other Charles spit out critical remarks when Bush talked about immigration, frivolous lawsuits, defense spending, social security, and going to Mars.

He almost blew up with disgust when the president talked about a National Endowment of Democracy, and he did explode with the president's comments about an Energy Act that backed a hydrogen economy. He stood up quickly, looked at Cathy and said: "May I?" Which was short for: "May I turn this off?"

She nodded her head, and Charles walked to the set and hit the power switch, not even considering use of the flipper.

He looked at Cathy, and in his firmest chemical engineering voice said: "The man has idiots for advisors. To make hydrogen by steam reforming or water gas shift produces 20% more carbon dioxide than if we burnt the fuel itself. The only other "electric" alternative to making hydrogen is to use nuclear power to generate the electricity, and that will never happen. Charles paused for a minute and then said: "It's a sham worse than Harken."

Cathy knew her husband was referring to the Harken Energy fiasco where Harvard money backed Harken in Middle East oil ventures that put shady dollars into Bush's pockets before the stock collapsed when little investors climbed aboard only to lose their shirts. Darryl Pickel, who handled all of the Weismantel Insurance, lost twenty-thousand dollars in the aftermath of deals that made Harken insiders rich and outsiders poor.

Charles looked directly at Cathy and said: "The man has no empathy for the little guy. He's an iceberg. The part of his plan that we don't see is costing the middle class a fortune." He walked into the kitchen, and from his voice she could tell his head was in the refrigerator as he screamed to her: "He's a damned FDR democrat."

Through it all, Charlie Junior had still managed to fall asleep. Cathy could no longer carry her son, so she urged him into an upright position and held on to him as they precariously toddled off to his bedroom. Charlie Junior was virtually sleepwalking while being guided by his mother.

Cathy knew she would not be sleeping soon because her GOP husband had become very upset with his political party and the failure of the elephants in the White House.

After tucking in CJ, she tiptoed downstairs and snuggled into the corner of the couch. Her husband hollered in from the kitchen: "Do you want part of my chocolate malt?"

"Sure, hon'," she replied, knowing it would be loaded with Hershey's syrup. The malt would be nice and thick, and it may have a raw egg in it. She heard the whirl of the Osterizer—Charles had insisted on buying the one with the glass—not plastic—container. Chuck appeared with two gigantic glasses, complete with long spoons and large-diameter straws. She began to listen to her husband's standard dissertation about the sham of the hydrogen economy.

CHAPTER FIVE
2016 – KILLING THE GOLDEN GOOSE: EXPORTING CAPITALISM

CJ banged his way through the front door carrying two large, heavy suitcases. His junior year – the hardest year in a chemical engineering program, was over. Cathy, looking frail, kissed him. She had run in from the kitchen, hands covered with flour because she had been kneading bread as her youngest had yelled from the porch: "Hi Honey, I'm home." As his mother kissed her son, his father looked at Charlie Junior and just starred at the boy-turned-man for a full few seconds and Charles could not believe what he was looking at.

– himself.

Charles had pulled out his high school scrapbook just yesterday and was looking at a picture of Number 41, the number he wore through four years of varsity basketball, and the face and body he saw on the toe head point guard in the newspaper-clipping-photo looked like the identical twin to his son........but........back to the present......

Charles said to himself: "They say if you want to see what your wife will look like in forty years, take a look at her mother, but, I didn't think it was true about father and sons – until right now."

"Welcome home, son." CJ had placed his big bags near the stairway and his dad gave him a bear hug. Charles was a huggy, touchy kind of guy with all the kids – and also with Cathy.

"Do you have…"

Right then and there, CJ's cell phone rang and he answered: "Speak to me."

It was Gerry.

Gerry White was a chum since third grade and, if by magic, Gerry always knew the exact moment Charlie Junior walked through the door.

Charles listened to the conversation long enough to know that Gerry's truck would be in the driveway in a few minutes. "Tell him to come over and have dinner." Everyone laughed and CJ adlibbed: "That goes without saying, Dad." Indeed, Gerry was a regular customer at the Weismantel dinner table, lunch table and breakfast table and he had no qualms of ever hiding his hearty appetite or grabbing something out of the refrigerator just as if he were at his own home.

Gerry arrived long before the two loaves of homemade honey wheat bread came out of the oven. Both Charles and the boys devoured one of the loaves as quickly as Cathy shook it from the bread pan. The full container of soft Fleishmann's oleo-margarine was consumed as quickly as the loaf with the melted drippings rolling off the hot slices all over the hands of the consumers. Every mouthwatering morsel was ravished by the men and the woman moaning the 'ummms and mmmm's that always accompany eating fresh baked bread. Not one of them wanted to wait to start the feast despite all the bread-eating rules to "let it cool" before cutting. That was impossible. Just like it is impossible to dunk and eat just one Oreo cookie.

Dinner was served on the patio, Luby's cafeteria-style, using the green metal table for the food although it was precariously placed next to the swimming pool. The talking centered on the boys and their upcoming senior year, but, then conversation took on serious intercourse – the economics outlook.

The value of the dollar against the Euro had reached an exchange rate of $1.00 U.S. dollars to 0.7 Euros....but....to the Weismantels (and Gerry) things were going to get a lot worse for the U.S. dollar before they got better. What really concerned Charles was the skyrocketing price of gasoline. He said: "If the Saudis lean toward using a basket of currency instead of the dollar, we are going to be paying $8.00 per gallon for gasoline."

The balance of payments deficit had jumped to over $4 trillion dollars (compared to $1.7 trillion in '05) with China, whose export of automobiles to the U.S. was challenging the Japanese. China held enough U.S. dollars to buy San Francisco given the '07 through '13 dip in real estate values.

CHAPTER SIX
2004 – APRIL

To save money, Charles and Cathy had planned to spend Tuesday night only in New Orleans and then to visit Maureapaux, LA and stay with Martha and Ted Ennis at their three-story home along the Amite River on Wednesday, perhaps getting in two hours of noodling at dusk. The Weismantels no longer noodled using competition standards because Charles, at his age, could no longer hold his breath very long.

So, he would dive, holding a long woven rope that had a big hook on one end. While Charles would find the fish and jam the hook into the fish's mouth and get out of the way of the flaying catfish, Cathy or Charlie Junior would haul the fish to the surface.

It worked!

And – it is one of the reasons that catfish frys at the Weismantel's were often and bountiful, with pounds and pounds of fillets. Neither husband nor wife ever revealed their catching secret, a secret that had been used in 1940s by Charles' father and uncle amidst overhanging rocks of the Medina River in

Bandera about 300 yards upstream from where the Route 173 bridge crosses the river.

The fishing plans and Ennis-visit were cancelled when Michelene Abboud invited them both to dinner on Wednesday night to meet Shaharon Shavell – an event that would impact their lives forevermore.

When in Louisiana, a favorite eating spot of the Weismantels was Pascal's Manale, and, a favorite dish was B-B-Q shrimp. And, while Cathy didn't think those shrimp were as good as her own shrimp or crawfish ettouffee, which she cooked often, tonight it was Pascal's Manale that was accepted by this group of four. Pascal's Manale was in the same location in New Orleans where it had been for years. The atmosphere and the bill-of-fare was the same as it was in 1940s—only the prices were different. The building was old. Could it withstand another Class 5? Doubtful!

The group started out by sitting at the oyster bar where Shaharon, with a great exclamation, discovered a pearl in one of his bakers dozen. It was a strange little gem, about the size of a pencil eraser and gorgeously, pearly, gemlike on one hemisphere, and like a bed rock on the other hemisphere. He treasured the discovery, however, despite the overall appearance of the virtually worthless stone, and Shaharon proclaimed that he would take it home and have it mounted for his wife – a thought that was totally Western in nature and obtuse for his Muslim faith and his Muslim wife, who dressed and practiced a traditional Islamic lifestyle.

At Pascal's Manale, Charles had noticed an unusual observer at the end of the oyster bar who did not seem to join in the excitement of the pearl discovery, and, who, to a great degree, seemed clandestine. This undercover attitude seemed strangely real when the observer – all alone – requested and occupied a table for four next to Charles, Michelene, Shaharon and Cathy. The stranger was alone, and, although many tables for two were readily available, he requested a table next to the Weismantel party. Furthermore, he appeared to be attentively attracted to each and every word that Charles uttered, and, when he left, slightly earlier than they did, Charles said: "Did any of you notice that the man sitting at the table next to us was gainfully employed at listening to our every word?"

Michelene looked at Shaharon with her head tilted downward, eyes lifted into her forehead while Shaharon glared directly into hers as if to say: "My worst fears have been realized." Neither of them said a word, but their silence said it all. The foursome was being monitored by the Department of Homeland Security. Indeed, after that dinner, both Charles and Cathy were monitored 24 hours per day for the rest of their lives.

Why?

Because Shaharon's strong technical talent in fluid-particle separation—especially centrifugation—made Shaharon a prime target to be monitored should anyone seek knowledge about uranium purification processing. Shaharon's association with anyone (this time it was Charles and Cathy) made these individuals suspect. Now the Weismantels were a concern ..... and ..... had become part of the CIA data bank.

CHAPTER SEVEN
2009 – BILDERBERG

"The rights of the individual come first!!" It was an emphatic statement coming from a thirteen-year-old, but he said it with such authority that many of those nearby who had not been listening to the conversation....began to listen.

The speaker was Charlie Junior Weismantel and CJ's comments were being addressed to Gerry White, CJ's lifelong buddy from Galveston. The White family had been living in Kingwood ever since Hurricane Katrina had damaged their island home. The White's would not be returning to Galveston for awhile, so, this school year allowed CJ and Ger to matriculate together at Kingwood High School, (KHS) ...and...both wore a mascot Mustangs logo as members of the KHS Academic Decathlon (AD) team.

It was during a lull in one of the AD study sessions (after hours at Kingwood High School) that the verbal ejaculation took place as CJ and Ger squared off in discussing the effects of the multi-trillion dollar debt that President Barak

Obama had inherited form George W. Bush and how Obama was pouring on much more red ink, adding to the national debt in quantum jumps, even worse than Reagan and both Bushes had done.

Sure, individual freedom was not a normal subject for teenagers – no more than they would normally be discussing Bobby Rush (cofounder of Black Panther Party in Illinois and now a Congressman) and his legislation for gun control (HR 45). But -- that was the kind of agenda that one would find on CJ's Daily Outlook Page. And – these topics were common for an AD team. Despite their age, neither AD contestants Weismantel or White were ashamed to present political or religious views that strayed from the norm. Neither boys were secularistic nor were they in favor of big government -- traits that they had inherited from their parents.

This inheritance stemmed from quietly listening to parental discussions – discussions that were often, and, often-in-detail. So, "the rights of the individual" comment by CJ (to Ger) was a normal reaction when the two of them heard an AD teacher's comment and quotation attributed to David Rockefeller who was supposed to have said: "All we need is the right crisis, and people will accept a New World Order." Both boys believed that the United States federal government already had too much power. This reflected a parental view that each had inherited.

Just last week the "fly on the wall" in CJ's room had heard him say to Gerry: "This is no longer a Democrat vs Republican issue – it is an issue of freedom of the individual vs government and big business, especially financial institutions and global corporations who are taking over our lives."

That kind of statement might raise the eyebrows of some of the KHS teachers as well as raise their ire. But -- CJ was merely reflecting family values – values that were:

- against too much government, and
- too much government-in-your-face,
- too much government control, and
- too much federal government spending
- in favor of moving decision-making to the lowest level of government, or, more specifically, to the family level.

However, returning to the reality of the moment, CJ, knew that his ejaculation had caught the eyes and ears of all nearby teachers and AD counselors and many students, So, he lowered his voice and, in a loud whisper to Ger, said: "Remember – it is no longer a Democrat vs Republican issue. But it is a states' rights issue."

With this, the AD leader stood and reacted with his own exclamation: "That's it for today." The room emptied and CJ and Ger went curbside to wait for their ride. Cathy could be seen ten cars in the distance, deep in the procession, yet, before one could utter "Jack Robinson" the teens were inside the car and soon being delivered home to the White's and home to the Weismantel's. Gerry's mom did not have pickup duty today because she – very pregnant -- had had a bad bout of morning sickness. Also, she was worried about catching the swine flew, but, more so, was worried about the baby in her womb (which they knew was a girl). That infant would be making her debut in early 2010.

When CJ got home, he immediately headed to his room and to his DELL INSPIRON that had been a Christmas present from his folks. He turned on the machine, criticized its version of Vista, and he Googled the words: Bilderberg Group. (That group had been part of the AD discussion of the day). He had never once heard of Bilderberg before today and was surprised to find a host of Bilderberg references .... over 315,000 .... to be more exact. This SEARCH had been stimulated by the discussion during the AD session that had centered on worldwide political influences such as The Rothschild's, China's Sovereign Fund, The Catholic Church and The Bilderberg Group. CJ had no idea of why Bilderberg had reached the discussion table, so he was checking it out.

CJ read his screen for a full forty minutes and then printed out Wiki info, being interrupted by his mothers call to him: "CJ, are you all right? You're awfully quite up there....dinner in ten minutes." He moved the mouse to SHUT DOWN and clicked the arrowed rodent, closed his portable DELL, and meandered down into the kitchen where his mom was boiling fresh-picked green pole-beans and his dad was reading the pink *Financial Times*. CJ asked:

"Dad, have you ever heard of the Bilderberg Group?"

A pin dropped and everyone heard it.

Charles looked at Cathy and she returned a silent stare, amazed at the question that their young son had raised. Charles asked CJ a question instead of immediately answering his son's inquiry. "Now where on earth did you experience a reference to The Bilderberg Group?" It was obvious that Charles knew of them.

"It came up in AD today," Charlie Junior replied.

Charles said: "Tell you what – let's eat some of your mom's pork roast and mashed potatoes and then have a big pow-wow after dinner to address your question properly." They all stood and went into the dining room and left Bilderberg in the kitchen .... But ... CJ had a lump in his throat in anticipation of what was going to be said after dinner. He could hardly swallow his mashed potatoes. But – before one could say "Jack Robinson" the three of them were all seated in the living room for the tutorial, that, dad would mostly deliver, with prompts from his better half. A couple times CJ's sibs walked through the room and Cathy simply shooed them away. They were not discussing something that was secret, but, Charles and Cathy knew that someday they would be putting certain family jewels into the hands of CJ, and this discussion was (even though CJ did not know it at the time) one of those periods of preparation that was special for their youngest child.

Both Cathy and Charles would elucidate as the evening wore on, but Charles began to speak.

"Son," Charles sternly addressed Charlie Junior....almost like they were in a courtroom, and, it was an unusual way for any father to speak to a young son so matter-of-factly as if the teenager were an adult. "When you bring up Bilderberg, you have hit on something that has been bothering your mother and me for some time." He paused .... and .... then Charles restarted the intercourse. "It is like this."

Years from this day, Charlie Junior would remember this tutorial and the three-hour dissertation that his father poured out from his heart, from his spleen, and from every organ essential to life. The message and the lesson-taught covered much more than Bilderberg ....It was a lesson in freedom, a lesson in the rights of the individual....a lesson in the hazards of a too-powerful a federal government, and a lesson on the dangers of what globalization can bring when coupled to a belief that there is good in a New World Order .... The latter, according to CJ's dad, was a blueprint for global enslavement. "Globalists," according to Charles, do not say this out loud, but believe in the adage: "I can always find a slave somewhere in the world who is willing to do a job to replace you."

For the individual to "see the light of day" and to understand what is happening to his or her freedom "is something the globalist cannot stand." The most important part of the lesson that CJ remembered was the emphasis that his parents placed on states rights and the rights of the family and the individual. Both his dad and his mother believed that, in the future, the federal government could and will use the army and other military branches against the states. This Weismantel conclusion came under the reign of George W. Bush who, on October 17, 2006, signed into law, a provision known as PUBLIC LAW 109-364 that gave the Federal Government the right to use the nation's armed forces against the civilian population in major public emergencies without consultation or input from governors. This order represented an unprecedented shift of power away from the states – a power that could prove catastrophic and deadly when placed in the hands of sovereign president.

It was with this background that CJ would recall what his father and mother had to say that day:

"CJ," his dad began, "There are a lot of myths about Bilderberg that you can find in book references and on the internet, but everything I am going to say to you today is based entirely on facts. And, the story starts with some of our, your mom and me, personal experiences.

"I am going to begin my stories with some background information that may not seem to be related to your original question, but each tidbit will help you understand some of the major influences that the US is experiencing, politically and financially, and who is behind the decision-making. If most people were aware of what is going on right under their noses, they would be up in arms......and.....that is an ironic statement for me to make given the current move in Congress to take away our arms.

"But -- I digress – let me get back on track.

"First, let's go back to 1974.....I officed with McGraw-Hill, the book publisher, and company that owns Business Week (BW) magazine, on the third floor of the California Teacher's Association (CTA) building. This building was near downtown Los Angeles on Wilshire Boulevard, and it was located just down the street from the headquarters of Signal Oil, now defunct, that was just down the street from the headquarters of Union Oil, now defunct, that was just down the street and just over the

Harbor freeway from Arco Oil and Gas, now defunct.

"It was 7:07 AM and I was outside the CTA building in the parking lot where delivery trucks bring in the day's ware. I was standing next to an ol' battered blue ice-truck with a Daily Racing Forum spread across the hood. I was 'figurin' a six-furlong race at Santa Anita, along with the owner of the truck—a 60-year-old-ice-man, who looked and acted like he was eighty, and, who somehow still delivered crushed and block ice to the basement cafeteria of the building. Dick Cleveland and I would meet at the same parking spot early every day –that is—early every day that the ponies were running. Why? Because we both had a love of the track and a tremendous desire to own our own thoroughbred. As we completed our study of the races, I handed Dick two dollars to bet (he was going out to the track) and I entered the building and then proceeded up the elevator to a darkened office – except – I could see way down the hall that the lights were on in the BW editorial office.

"Tom Self was the Regional Editor for BW, and he was never in the office that early, so the light being on was obtuse. Tom may decide to get up to play golf at that time of the day – say -- at the Wilshire Country Club, but, to be in the office was obscene.

"I hollered loudly; 'Tom! .....Are you here?' There was a grumbling response, so I walked down to peek in the door and there he was....as bedraggled and bearded as a bum could be, sitting on the floor shuffling through old back issues of his rag. I looked at him and said: 'What in the world are you doing here at this hour of the day?' He looked up at me and grunted: 'I'll buy you a cup of coffee and tell you all about it.'

"Tom and I headed to the basement cafe, hooked up with two cups of black, and took seats at a corner table. Not all of the lights were on, and this table, being away from the serving counter, became an ideal place for a stealthy conversation.

"I gave Tom the podium, and he took it immediately.

"I was watching Johnny Carson," he said, "and just as I was about to turn off the lights and call it a day, the phone rang. I asked myself: Who would be calling me at this devilish hour? To my surprise, it was Justin Dart.

"Now, to put this in perspective, there used to be a major drug store and pharmacy chain called Rexall. They had outlets all over the country and also had a presence in plastics, and were headquartered in LA. Dart was the President of Rexall and ruled the company with an iron hand – and – stockholders loved the return and dividend that was paid. So, they changed the name of the company to Dart Industries.....Today that is part of someone else, but, in '74, they were a powerful company ..... as was Dart himself.....in fact.....Dart was one of the most important Republicans in Southern California.....and...as Tom Self was a Republican, (in those days this tag was a bit unorthodox for an editor), Dart and Self knew one another and probably had the same handicap.

"Justin told Tom that he wanted Tom to come over to his house right away, and the invitation, according to Tom, who was telling me the story, was not accepted with alacrity, but with disdain, Yet, it was accepted -- accepted, because Dart sugared the invite with the words:

'We are going to elect a president.' .... and .... no editor could go to sleep with that kind of comment on his mind. So....Tom motored over to Justin Dart's, arriving near midnight.

"Dart himself answered the door and immediately placed a drink in Tom's hand while Tom inquired: 'What is this all about?' Dart replied: 'You'll see.' And, as Tom looked around the room he told me that he saw people he knew to be the most powerful and rich Republicans in the State of California ...... businessmen........car dealers....... politicos .... and ... as he reviewed the clan, he was told: 'Tom, we are going to elect a president, and we want you here to tell us how we can handle the media. Indeed, Tom Self was godlike when it came to understanding the workings of the fourth estate ...... which .... as Edmund Burke so rightfully put it 'is more important than them all.'

"Not 10 minutes later, in walked the candidate -- Ronald Reagan.

"Tom iterated to me how he had been up all night contributed to the planning of what had to be done to get Reagan elected, and when...what it would cost...which editor or broadcaster was friendly....and ... who was not...he addressed what spin had to be prepared....and on and on and on. It was a lesson for me and it was extremely eye-opening in respect to the inside working of the making of a president.

"Son, I told you this story because I want you to understand that there are smoke-filled rooms, clandestine meetings and political players tied to corporate money .... worse today than in 1974. The stakes are much bigger today as one can attest to the trillions of dollars handed out by George Bush ... and ... these dollar giveaways have been exacerbated under Obama. But, one can look at real numbers and see that it was Republicans that initiated most of the spending and the red ink ....at least until this year.

"For sure, the Bilderberg Group (BG) has an influence on what is and has been happening in financial and economic circles ... but ... they are just one of the influential entities such as The Skull and Bones (S&B) organization at Yale University, The Federal Reserve Bank (FRB), the Institute for Public Studies (IPS), and the Council of Foreign

Relations (CFR). These organizations, and some others, all have somehow attained an unquestionable legitimacy in the press, with many politicians and businessmen finding a home in several of these organizations. There are puppeteers, however, and these people holding the strings are elated when their 'boys' will definitely be in the presidential drivers seat. This was the case when John Kerry (S&B) ran against George Bush (S&B) .... and .... as far back as 1952 when Dwight Eisenhower (CFR) ran against Adali Stevenson (CFR). More recently, Gerald Ford (S&B and BG) provided interlocking information that deserves more attention. But for now, I know you want me to address Bilderberg."

"So that you will know, I use the name *The Omega Group* to address the matrix of all puppeteers. And, son, let me emphasize, that I am NOT suggesting some big conspiracy theory...I am only telling the story as it actually exists ... a story that deals with factual financial influences and political influences .... Influences we must address if we are to maintain our freedoms under the Constitution and the Bill of Rights.

"In that light, you have always heard me say: 'Follow the dollars and you will see how and where the influences lie.' This suggests the need that a very close look at the FRB is in order …and …that assessment would be correct … but … today we will look at Bilderberg, which, as you suspected, does deserve close attention."

"Everyone knows about the birth of The Bilderberg Group. The catalyst and promoter of their first meeting was Prince Bernhard of the Netherlands, who, at the suggestion of Joseph Retinger, and with the support of powerful banking interests, namely, the Rockefellers and the Rothschilds, called together a group of elite guests by-invitation-only to address issues related to the financial system, politics, military issues and education. The name came from the location of the first meeting place: Hotel de Bilderberg, Oosterbeek, the Netherlands.

"By the by, the prince got caught with his hand in the cookie jar in respect to sales of military equipment. The debacle included US companies, and while I recall that this was a shameful situation, the illegalities did not take him down.

"But—back to Bilderberg.....While critics point to the secrecy of events at the Group's meetings, some information does leak out. For example, it has been established that, under the Bush administration Bilderbergers have been moving generally toward a goal of business globalization and, specifically, a North American Union. It is this latter focus that has me worried, and here is why.

"Mom and I took a very close and serious look at the NAFTA agreement. I ordered and received a complete copy of the actual document as it was being proposed, and, when the document arrived, I unpacked a stack of papers that was almost two feet high. I dug into reading the document—or—at least skimming it until I came across something important.

"I remember coming home one night...."

Cathy abruptly interrupted Charles' sentence saying: "And I asked him point blank—well—what did you find?"

"And—I answered—'You are not going to believe it.'"

"What your dad found out was that almost the entire document was made up of boiler plate that hid job movement plans of high paying jobs from the United States to other parts of the world, and ..... "

"And,"....continued, Charles, "I told mom that the hang up in passing NAFTA was totally related to the section on the banking industry. I said: 'As soon as the banking industry gets what they want, the legislation will pass with flying colors ...and...that is precisely what happened."

Cathy said: "Dad likened NAFTA to the frontier moving West....The scheme was to create a North American Union whereby Mexico could be bought up by the banks for ten cents on the dollar...and...years from now be sold to Americans for ten dollars a square foot, just like some parts of the hill country was priced at twenty-five cents per acre back in the 1930's."

"And, what is the Bilderberg interface?" asked Charles Junior.

Cathy looked at Charles, and in unison they answered their son's question with one word.

"MONEY!!"

CHAPTER EIGHT
2022 – FORMERLY A SECRETARY

He was much older now and the years had not been good to him. As a key member of the presidential cabinet, he had not been blamed totally for the debacle in Iraq, but he, along with the woman who replaced him, Condolica Rice, were not loved by the American public...then or now...not even by the minorities. His hair was still crew cut only now it was totally gray, or totally white, one might say. It was a vivid contrast to his brown skin, and, as the TV cameras panned the panel of old soldiers, Charlie Junior watched and listened attentively to the retired general who had been President George W. Bush's first Secretary of State.

Charlie Junior carried the weight of death on his shoulders having lost his dad only two months ago. And now that both Cathy and Charles were in heaven, their goals and traditions were left to him, their youngest son, who had his parents' ideals embedded in his mind and in his heart. In that regard he was ever vigilant to the government's encroachment on personal freedom. He knew that he was now the one being monitored 24 hours a day. In his dying breath Charles made Charlie Junior pledge the family's allegiance to a resistance to any federal action that would give the military any more power over the populous. "Protect us from our government," were Charles' last words.

Today's TV forum, organized by GEORGE (the acronym), was titled: **Funding More Military Power**. The focus was employing more military strength at home and in the Middle East...the antithesis of Weismantel thinking.

Five current or former generals made up the panel and George Stephanopoulos, himself graying, was the host and monitor in front of editors-in-chief from Newsweek, Business Week, The New York Times, Washington Post and The Conservative. The Conservative had been founded after the 2008 presidential election to foster the idea of small government, a balanced budget and a strong belief in The Bill of Rights. Charlie Junior was a charter subscriber because he believed the Republican Party had abandoned those goals.

Stephanopoulos started the exchange with a tough, no holds barred question to all five generals: "Why weren't we prepared for the aftermath of hostility after the war with Iraq? And why are we still there? And when will we get out?" He fired the questions like an old Browning Automatic Rifle.

Three of the panel fumbled with five-minute answers that almost seemed like they believed it was our right to be in there...it was their job to be there. They defended the inhuman actions at U.S. prisons in Iraq, Guantanamo, and elsewhere around the world, while acknowledging that torture, such as waterboarding, had approval from the CIA, FBI, AG, and even the president.

The UN resolution condemning the United States' use of torture never got past the Security Council.

Then Powell asked for the podium. And – his short, twenty word reply stunned Charlie Junior with its candid accuracy. Powell said, "We were prepared to handle things like in France after World War II. Instead we should have been planning for insurgency."

Yes, CJ was stunned. Thousands of Americans had lost their lives in a war built on non-substantiated evidence, many of them in skirmishes with Persian troops who dipped in and out of the Southeast Regions of the country. These in-and-out sorties were supported by both Iraqi and Iranian Shiites urged to terrorism by clerics who promoted the assurance of heaven for those who died the martyr's death. Scores of American prisoners, both civilian and military, had suffered cruel beheading on video tape. The beheadings were often tied to Al Qaeda or to marauding groups of Sunis who had gone undercover after losing virtual all of their rights after the latest Iraqi national election, or, the marauders were Shiites following hawkish religious leaders. AND—the horrendous errors of Iraq had been repeated over and over in Afghanistan.

The U.S. had never fought such a war for so long, with so little success and no hope for an end in sight.

Godlessly, the war and deaths had moved onto U.S. soil with mini-nine-elevens occurring so often that now, anyone with an Islamic name was treated with disgust and irreverence.

Michelene Abboud, a Lebanese Christian, had lost her tenure at a Southern university over a publication incident involving a technical paper delivered at the World Engineering Congress held last year in Belgium. Her coauthor had been Shaharon Shavell, a Muslim. Being directly associated with a Muslim was all it took to ruin her years of dedication to many engineering students.

Detroit, a haven for the Islamic religion in the U.S. since the late 1980s, was a burning coal of hatred and violence, especially if an Islamic individual was black. KKK-type activity was common in Detroit, and burning crosses had been placed in a Muslim cleric's yard near Grosse Point Parke.

CJ flipped the channel to seek a more humorous program but could not find one worth watching after five second viewing stops at twenty-four different channels. He pressed the power button off and the picture disappeared ending in a thousand points of light turning dark.

He picked up the phone and called the cell phone of his best friend, Gerry White.

"Whatcha doin'," he said, without identifying himself when Gerry answered. Gerry knew CJ's voice immediately. He had been hearing that voice his entire life. Besides—he had programmed CJ's number to ring in as the Alleluia Chorus. Unmistakably it was CJ calling.

"I'm over with Mom and Dad," he replied, "and we are about to sit down to about 100 stuffed cabbages..." he paused..."and a dozen of them have your name written on them."

CJ said: "I'll be right over!" In less than 90 seconds the top on the Mustang convertible exposed CJ's hair to the Houston sunlight and he rode 350 horses to Galveston.

Driving the Beltway, Charlie Junior began to think about stuffed cabbage. Mrs. White was born on the Pest side of the river in Budapest. Her Hungarian heritage clung to her despite years of exposure to Texas. Her European prowess in the kitchen was unmatched. CJ easily succumbed to the heavy, hearty, Hungarian sauces that Mrs. White always said were low calorie. She said the same thing about her homemade twelve-layer Dobosh Torte, and as vision of such vittles raced through his mind, the memory was so mouth watering that Charlie Junior raced well above the speed limits South on I-45 to reach his dinner destination much more quickly than expected. He walked into the four-story White home on Eighth Street, just down from the Old Bishop's Mansion, in less than an hour.

He walked in the front door without knocking, just as he had been doing since he was talkative toe head. The Whites and the Weismantels had been friends for years and Gerry's folks were CJ's godparents.

When he entered, Alveta, Gerry's twelve-year-old sister, ran up to him and hugged him yelling: "CJ will you marry me?" That phrase had become the family joke because Alveta had been saying that to Charlie Junior ever since she was four-years-old.

CJ smiled at her and replied: "Soon as you grow up!" And – they both laughed.

Charlie Junior made his way into the kitchen, high-fived Gerry and went to the sink where Mrs. White stood washing fresh, dark, red beets just pulled from the garden. He hugged her and looking at the stove, he said to Gerry: "You weren't kidding." Indeed, there on the stove were two large turkey roasters, lined wall-to-wall with stuffed cabbages. There were easily one hundred.

Mrs. White pulled down the oven door and unbelievably there were another forty or so in a baking dish.

Charlie Junior hollered in jubilation, "yoi eesh ta nen!!" in a language that was supposed to be Hungarian.

CHAPTER NINE
2022 – SAN JACINTO RIVER

Just before his dad died – Charlie Junior was 26 at the time – his father had warned him of how the trouble in Iraq would be imported back to the States. It was one chilly morning in April when just the two of them took the little flatboat [somewhere in size between a perot and a Johnboat] out into the San Jacinto River where they were running three trot lines. They were using a heavy-duty, knit line that had been smothered and smeared in a coal-tar resin to keep it from rotting under continual use. The hooks were about thirty feet apart, each hook having its own snap swivel for easy removal if they wanted to move the line....they never moved the line with hooks on.

Charles had packed up an ice chest full of breakfast goodies and the two of them headed for a special spot called "The Point" – a peninsula just below the Atascocita bridge that was somewhat secluded. It pointed the way toward Lake Houston and had a large sand bar at the tip. Very few people ever reached or walked that cloistered beach on the South side of the river, but it was a favorite, isolated stopping point for Charles and Charlie Junior before entering the lake.

It was Lee Boudreaux, their next door neighbor, a displaced Cajun from Lafayette who worked undercover for the INS, who first called that sandbar "The Point." The name had stuck.

Lee who was the only person Charlie Junior had ever known who had been ambushed by a hit man, and Lee had killed the hitter. The Mexican mafia had a bounty on Lee, who told CJ: "Don't ever come into the house unannounced; I shoot through the bedroom doors with a Colt 45 using a flathead bullet." Charlie Junior knew that kind of bullet would blow a man's chest apart.

Ninety out of one hundred illegals coming across the Rio Grande knew Lee by name and by reputation. Hundreds had felt the steel of his cuffs, and if there was a mystery about Lee, it was how he had remained alive despite the bounty on his head. Lee had captured many a Mexican, or Central American, even when they had attacked him with boca knives. These are the knives about three times the size of a tile knife that have a large, sharp, curved hook at the end. One swipe would tear a man's guts out...or...a woman's.

And—if an illegal could not kill him, Lee's wild spirit might accomplish what no illegal could do. One night, drunk to a level of 0.4 or more, Lee, on a dare, was lowered by rope down an old, dry water well where "buddies" had thrown three rattlesnakes. With an Astros hat on his head, he swore he could catch one of the snakes bare handed.

Why five grown men, all officers of our boarder patrol, would lower one of their own down into that snake pit is a question best not asked. But—down he went hollerin' and yellin': "Down, down, down," ....and....in a split instant: "Up, up, up." ..... and .... when they pulled him out of the hole he was hatless and holding a four foot rattler in his hand. These kind of true stores spread across both sides of the border from Tijuana to Brownsville.

Lee had told CJ the snake story on several occasions as well as the secret to his success. "The snake," says Lee, "always strikes at heat. So, I took my hot hat off and threw it toward the snakes, and all three rattlers struck. I simply grabbed the closest one because, after they are extended, they are not coiled to strike again."

CJ never asked nor did he understand how Lee could see and catch a rattler in the dark, especially after drinking most of bottle of Jose Cuervo. But, CJ always figured that it was just part of the legend.

However, on that chilly morning in April when Charles and Charlie Junior headed down river to The Point, CJ was not thinking of Lee Boudreaux. He was asking himself why his dad had told him to block out the whole morning...so...Charlie Junior had blocked out the whole day.

After seining for shad to bait the trotlines, they sped the Johnboat to The Point and in fifteen minutes a fire was going on the sand and the smell of maple-flavored bacon filled the air.

Charlie Junior wondered whether alligators liked bacon because one time he and Lee spotted a big ol' 'gator right about the place they were breakfasting today.

"Rule Number One:" Lee had explained: "Never get between the alligator and the water. Rule Number Two: never be holding on to something that an alligator wants to eat. Rule

Number Three: remember that alligators can run fast – faster than you can run."

One night, quite awhile ago, Boudreaux came over to the house about an hour after dark and whispered to CJ, "Let's go get that alligator tonight. We'll use your canoe." He was dead serious and carried a half-inch rope, an ax and a flashlight." It took only a Rhode Island second for Charlie Junior to say "No" to that idea.

But, on <u>this</u> April morning—one of the last outings he would ever spend with his dad— there was no alligator in sight and the bacon and eggs were hot off the fire and being spatula-ed onto the metal camping plates. Breakfast was served. Father and son sat down on two sturdy canvas camping stools, the ones that look like an "x" if you see them from the side, and CJ said: "Do you think the coffee's ready?"

"Sure is." Charles replied, and CJ got up, went to the fire and poured two cups. He called this "sludge coffee" because you boiled water and ground coffee all together and simply decanted the liquid off the top. There was always sludge in the bottom of the cup, and the

64

secret was to stop drinking one half inch before you reached the bottom.

Charlie Junior handed the tin canteen cup to his dad and then dad cleared his throat and spit out the clearing, washing his throat pipe with the hot brew. He could feel the heat reach all the way down to his duodenum.

"Son," he said, "I brought you out to The Point for a reason." He paused and said, "What do you see?"

CJ looked around. "Nothin'," he replied.

"Exactly," Charles said. "Nothing!" Then he added: "That's just the way I wanted it." The two of them considered their position and the view along each of 2π radians.

Indeed, if you flew North from The Point as the crow flies, you flew over the river, over a quarter mile of woods, and eventually reached the Deerwood Golf Course.

Looking East the view included mostly water, the mouth of the river, Lake Houston, and over two miles away the East bank of the Lake Houston where there was still no development.

Behind them and West were the peninsula, woods, and more woods. One would have to travel several miles before reaching civilization.

South of them was a long finger of the river bound by The Thicket on both sides of the finger. There were no roads and, having run trotlines on both sides of the finger for several years, both men knew there was nary a path from shore to anywhere. It was deer country, nutria territory, and blackberry thickets...the little, sour kind of blackberry....not the good ones.

Overhead an occasional plane passed over on its way to Runway Three at IAH. The Point lay directly under that approach to Bush Intercontinental. There was no Omnirange in site, so the only view of the two men—if someone wanted to see them—might be by satellite, and that was possible, but not probable.

"This is one of the few places where nothing we say will be heard," Charles said.

"Unless the boat is bugged," CJ laughed.

Then, in all seriousness his dad said: "Son, I've been over the boat with a fine tooth comb. There is no bug. I've checked every inch."

Charlie Junior looked at his dad. He knew this was something big.

Two hours later, Charlie Junior knew the family secret.

CHAPTER TEN
2068 – THE POINT REVISITED

Charlie Junior had just celebrated his 72nd birthday but he was so active and as sharp today as he was twenty years ago. He didn't noodle for catfish anymore and had quit running trotlines when Lee Boudreaux moved back to Louisiana. But he still was on the river, any river in Texas where he could catch crappie or white bass. He was a meat fisherman to this day, and while Chuck was a catch-and-release, largemouth man, they both enjoyed *Outside*. In fact they relished reading the magazine with that name.

At 26, Chuck had taken over the family business after graduating magna cum laude from UT Austin in 2062. Following the family tradition, his sheepskin was recorded as a BS degree in Chemical Engineering. He loved visiting the campus and the ChE Building, often bragging a bit that his grandfather had contributed greatly to the university.

Chuck had never known Charles, his grandfather, nor had he known his grandmother, Cathy. Both had died long before his dad and mom were married. In fact, Chuck acted as his own mother, being only four when Alveta died. Chuck remained lovingly close to both his sisters who feverishly tried to fix him up with blind dates, but, like his dad, it appeared he was not going to be married early in life.

Also, Chuck was intertwined like a mesh with each uncle and aunt – all who had a keen interest in White Cloak, the family coatings business, because the company still provided a quarterly dividend to each family member...a dividend that was not growing.

Up until now, Chuck had devoted full attention to building back the business that had been devastated by the growth of imported paints from China, something Chuck could not understand because the quality of these paints was terrible. There was always the fear that these paints contained lead, a fact that Mattel Toy Company learned in 2007. The company is still living with their lack of quality control. So—

When the phone rang late last night and his dad, Charlie Junior, suggested breakfast at The Point, Chuck did not realize that – along with the tradition of maple-bacon and eggs – he would be given the keys to family secrets that had worked their way from Charles and Cathy, through Charlie Junior and Alveta and now would become his.

Chuck did not hitch his 20-foot bass boat to his Durango, but drove over to his dad's knowing they would use the old Johnboat. He opened his dad's garage door with his own electric garage door opener, dismounted and entered the house by walking through the garage. He walked by the old Mustang convertible, still in immaculate condition admiring this peace of American nostalgia that would someday be in his garage. Charlie Junior had built extra security measures both in his garage and in Chuck's. Today Chuck would learn why.

Chuck passed through his dad's utility room...it was a mess...the whole house was a mess with the messes of a widower.

His dad heard him enter and yelled from the upstairs bedroom: "Hi son, can you put the food and tackle into your truck; it's right there by the back door."

Indeed, the fishing gear, shining with new monofilament, was ready to go, as was two full Kroger bags of breakfast booty.

His dad yelled: "Will you hook up the Johnboat trailer to the truck?"

"Ok!"

"See you in the car," Chuck responded. He didn't like referring to the Durango as a truck, although he still talked about the engine as a hemi. That was the buzz word again—just like it had been during the millennium year. Within minutes, the craft was in the water and they were puttering down the San Jacinto River toward The Point.

Chuck knew The Point of the river as well as he knew his own driveway. He probably had logged more time on that part of the San Jacinto than anyone alive. He followed the deep part of the channel which was sometimes starboard, sometimes not, and, almost at full throttle, the new Mohawk engine sent the bow into a bouncing mode. If one did not know this river, a tree submerged six inches below the surface of the water would easily tear the boat apart.

They arrived at The Point without stopping to net shad, and Charlie Junior had fired up the portable burner to make sludge coffee even before the boat was secure.

"I love coming to The Point," Chuck said. "It is still so secluded."

"Indeed, yes indeed," the 72-year-old CJ replied.

Charlie Junior had taken up bird watching two years ago after coming across and buying a battered old book called: *The Banner Year.* He didn't travel across the country and spend a fortune to find fowl, but he did make it a point to list all the species he saw on the San Jacinto. He even posted a "bird list" in the Deerwood locker room where members could list their own name, and then they could add information about the bird, such as class, genius and species. The bird they saw had to have been on the river or the golf course when they saw it, and members were supposed to list where they saw it. This idea caught on quite well and had actually spread to other golf courses across the United States.

Ironically, right now, as the sound of burning propane sent BTUs to the bottom of the beaten ol' coffee pot, a bird sent out its call.

"Listen," he said to Chuck. "I can't see it, but that is definitely a black-throated cardinal...did you know they spend the winter in the Yucatan and fly over the entire Gulf of Mexico to High Island before resting, eating and continuing their migration?"

"No, I didn't know that, Dad."

Chuck watched his dad walk over to the boat and examine it, every inch of it. Charlie Junior then returned to the fire and flame and he fried the bacon and basted the eggs. Breakfast was as beautiful as it was bountiful, and the old man then sat back in a brand new aluminum lawn chair and looked at his son quite seriously.

"Chuck," he said, "I have a confession to make to you. I think it is something you already suspect, but now you must understand everything."

Then CJ handed his son a rod and reel saying: "Let's talk while we are drowning worms."

CHAPTER ELEVEN
2082 – THE PAINT FACTORY I

First, Charles had been a dynamically successful engineering consultant. Then, he and Cathy started "White Cloak Paint & Lacquers" in their garage, literally. CJ joined the business even before graduating from UT Austin, and when Chuck entered the picture, he became the third generation of chemical engineers in the Weismantel family to manage the company.

Like his dad, Chuck had finished the four year program at UT in 3-1/2 years. He was only 20 years old when he accepted the valedictorian medal for the engineering college. That was 2062. Now, at 40-years old, Chuck pretty much ran the company, but his dad, who was still called Charlie Junior or CJ after all these years, came in each day and stayed very late. This was a habit he formed after Alveta died. Chuck always joined his dad for the late hour trabajo after the quality control chemists left the premises after finishing QC procedures for the day's batches. When that door closed, the plant was virtually quiet except for the 24-hour-a-day deep-rolling noise of the ancient steel ball mills that were still used to grind very hard pigments, like iron blue and brown iron oxide.

The "White Cloak" factory was a three-story maze of nooks and crannies, which surprisingly was modeled after the old GMG factory in San Francisco at 1019 Mission Street that was built eons ago in 1910. Raw materials were delivered by backing semi-tractor trailer trucks up a steep ramp. This led to gravity-assisted movement of all liquid and solid products until the finished paint reached the filling lines on the ground floor which there led to a gigantic warehouse that was totally automated. Robots could pick and choose from shelving that was over three stories tall. Conveyors fed boxes of paint to a gathering area where they were automatically stacked under the supervision of a single person. At one time, eighteen people had been employed in warehousing to pick orders. Now, there was a $30 million inventory and all shipping was the job of one man. All this was possible by using an integrated warehousing system called HAWKEYE Perfect Measuring. This was a data synchronization system tied to dimensional weight, warehouse cubing and space management.

This single person had two assistants, one real and one mechanical. The mechanical was the HAWKEYE Perfect Measuring System for determining dimensional weight, and the other was a person who moved finished goods from the factory into the warehouse. The latter had one of the most critical jobs in the plant; inventory replacement was critical if automation was to work. Almost from the beginning White Cloak had tied its coding system to the international UCCnet and its GS-1 offshoot. Additionally, White Cloak had adopted the latest radio frequency bar coding technology.

White Cloak automation preceded the quantum jump in scanning adopted by Wal-Mart. Back around the turn of the century, the company had a forward-looking MIS manager that Wal-Mart eventually hired and he—the White Cloak alum—eventually became Wal-Mart's president.

At that time, Wal-Mart called in all of their suppliers and presented a mandate: "In seven years all Wal-Mart products must carry a Radio Frequency Bar Code, given the acronym,

RFBC." The idea behind this was to eliminate as many employees as possible at the checkout stand. Customers would simply roll their baskets through an opening – like those that scan airplane passengers before entering the gate area – and – low megahertz scanners would immediately identify everything in the customer's basket and provide a printout that was preferably paid for by a debit card. Wal-Mart did not want to handle cash – due to the potential mistakes – or credit cards – due to fees.

Since the turnover goal of all products in the store was two weeks, and Wal-Mart paid its bills in 60 to 90 days, this meant billions of dollars of free inventory rested on Wal-Mart shelves and in the warehouse as a "float". Because checks accepted by Wal-Mart or on a person's debit card immediately deposited the customer's money in Wal-Mart's bank account, this gave Wal-Mart the use of several billion dollars for about 60 days. In effect, Wal-Mart had become a cash-rich banker with virtually no financial exposure. All inventory was virtually on consignment because Wal-Mart would return merchandise that didn't move at a prescribed turnover rate.

In two decades Wal-Mart had reduced their number of employees by 50% while the company grew four-fold, and the CFO was the most critical job in the whole company. Some CFOs, when they have overnight cash, will invest it for 24 hours. Wal-Mart's float allowed them to place $60 Billion (of someone else's money) for 60 days in a constant turnover. They were effectively robbing their suppliers of that interest by not paying them promptly, and, customers paying by check pay instantly because the store didn't even keep the check. They hand it back to you after debiting your account. CJ had been in the middle of setting up the system. In fact—

"White Cloak" had preempted the Wal-Mart need. They were one of the first companies to adopt RFBC. White Cloak became bedfellows with Wal-Mart and the fallout was that "White Cloak" itself reduced its employment and became a showplace of how a debit system should work. It became a state-of-the-art example of that system.

Ironically, White Cloak still operated under the old adage of 10%, 10 days.

But in terms of employment, what no one knew was that the Weismantels had good reasons and anxieties to have fewer people around the production facilities. <u>Very</u> secret products were being made right under GEORGE's eyes.

The security arms of the government suspected something, but neither frequent OSHA visits nor EPA cops could ever find anything obtuse. No one had any idea of what was taking place in front of their noses.

There were two reasons why Charlie Junior had inherited White Cloak Paint, Varnish & Lacquer LLC when Charles died ten years ago. Even though CJ was the youngest child, he was the only one of the seven siblings who really wanted to run the company. Also, he was the only one who pursued a chemical engineering career like his mom and dad and thus knew how to run the company.

Charles and Cathy built the company from zero up to $40 million, and Charlie Junior, mainly through internal growth and sales of high-value, high-margin nitrocellulose products, now owned a $100 million company. Well, at least he owned all the voting stock. The parents had created a second class of profit-sharing stock for the other six children, so, everyone was happy to let Charlie Junior send them a quarterly dividend check. CJ was going to do something similar when he had a family, but, as the new year began, he was so married to his work, that he hardly ever dated.

With Friday evening starring him in the face, CJ sat in his office in the big leather chair in front of the antique roll-top desk, placed his hands behind his neck, leaned back and asked himself: "I wonder if the dogs are racing tonight?" Gulfstream Park in Texas City was a hub for him and Gerry, and, then, as if by magic, the phone rang and it was Gerry. Gerry spoke first, even before CJ could say: "Bueno" in gringo Spanish.

"How you doin' bro?" Indeed they had been like brothers all of their lives, so it was not unusual for Gerry to say "bro." Gerry often referred to Charlie Junior as brother, or "bro" for short.

"Just sittin' here thinking about you and the dogs," CJ quipped.

White re-quipped: "Do you mean racing dogs—or the losers that I date?" They both laughed.

Gerry said, "Why don't you come down and spend the night. Tomorrow we're having a birthday party for Alveta, and you can be my present to her." Then he added: "Besides, I have a half-off coupon for Landry's....Let's eat"

"You're on," CJ replied. "What time?

"What time can you make it for dinner?"

"Six o' six."

"Okay – I'll meet you at the house and will let Sissy be the designated driver." Alveta, in Southern tradition was often referred to as Sissy by both her brother and Charlie Junior. In four minutes, CJ's black Mustang's 350 horses were hummin' toward Galveston.

CJ pulled up to the house about 5:45 PM and honked. Gerry damned near stumbled as he hurried down the front stairs of the White's home. There were fourteen stairs leading up to the front porch. The stairs were old, they were steep, and usually friends entered through the back door to avoid them.

Gerry opened the passenger door of the top-down convertible and said: "How long are you going to keep this thing?"

"ForEVer," he replied.....with as much emphasis on EV as he could.

They sat there, waiting for Alveta. Charlie Junior had not seen her much for five years since she went away to Stanford and graduated last year. She had stayed in California to work a year with Dream Works doing computer animation.

She popped out the front door, maneuvered the stairs like a skier side-slipping and leaped to the door on the driver's side landing at the open window kneeling with her face directly into CJ's.......their noses were not five inches apart.

"Will you marry me?" she said.

Charlie Junior took one look at her and was mesmerized by her beauty. After all these years she had grown up...she had really grown up. She was gorgeous!

For once, Charlie Junior could *not* give his glib: "Soon as you grow up" answer.

There she was, five foot eight inches tall, a body that could win the Miss America title, blond, blue eyes, a smile that would melt a man's heart, joyful, smart, affable and she had just asked him to marry her....just like she had been doing since she was four years old.

Yes, he knew it was their standard joke, but he did not miss the moment. He said, "Really, Alveta, its time for me to ask the question: Will *you* marry me?"

Gerry jerked his head around and his jaw dropped onto the floor mat. He didn't say anything but watched the drama unfold. He knew CJ really meant what he had said...and...it was being said to *his* baby sister.

Alveta was still face-to-face with CJ. If she was stunned by his question she lived through it totally unnerved, almost like she had been waiting for it...............waiting for years.

She leaned over and kissed him right on the lips with the most loving, intimate, Frenchless tease. She shouted: "Yes!" because she *had* been waiting eighteen years for this day.

Alveta hopped into the back seat of the convertible without opening the door, just like a tennis pro hopping the net after a victory. She stuck her head between the two "brothers" and said to Gerry: "You can close your mouth, Ger. You should have known it was inevitable. Let's go eat and celebrate. I'm engaged."

Her words were like music. Dumfounded, Charlie Junior realized he had proposed to a woman he had never dated but whom he had loved for years.

CHAPTER THIRTEEN
2047 – THE PAINT FACTORY III

Charlie Junior sat in the big leather chair in front of the antique roll-top desk, placed his hands behind his neck, leaned back, and looked at the 8 x 10 photograph of the woman he loved, the mother of three and the most loving woman who had ever lived. She had died a year ago today, July 1, unthinkable, at the young age of 36. CJ was lost without her as was little Chuck, who, had just finished toddling and was still asking: "Where's Mommy, Daddy?"

CJ was 50 now, and kept asking: "Why did God take her first?"

He knew he had to beat the depression that forced itself into his daily routine if only to give a positive face to his two daughters and to Chuck.

To make matters worse, imports from China were eating away at White Cloak's business and raw material prices had skyrocketed. Half the chemical plants on the Houston ship channel sat there, idle, and there was no plan by anyone to dismantle the rusting, obsolete tanks and towers, some filled with toxic and hazardous materials of bankrupt chemical process plants and oil refineries closed down due to the lack of crude oil. He picked up an article that his father had written for the Houston Business Journal many years ago. It was titled:

The Dangers of Democracy

Winston Churchill had several criticisms of democracy, but he always felt it was better than the alternatives. One wonders how he would feel today, where the majority may rule, but the majority (and their elected officials) are following ideals that are morally and ethically wrong—and—one can question integrity and values—like believing that torture is OK.

Both as a businessman and as a citizen, I would like to suggest that trends in governmental policy and governmental action are, frankly, terrifying. For those of us who believe in liberty, the United States Federal Government has gone on a

regulation spree—in the name of protecting the people against terrorism—when—de facto, we need to be worried about how to protect ourselves against the government. The problem is much more than allowing lead paints enter the country on children's toys, finding residual volatile organic compounds in imported polyester soda-pop bottles, or allowing tainted Chinese-grown chicken to enter the country as dog food that could lead to an outbreak of a massive bird flu epidemic.

There are a host of other concerns today, brought about by a president and a cadre of his supporters that have spent more, and earmarked more money than any administration in the history of the United States, all the while promoting more and more regulations while citizens lose more and more freedoms while being watched by both private companies and by government agencies. The watching is by personal observation, electronic transaction monitoring, wire tapping and cell phone listening-in. There are dangers all around us, not just from bomb threats but by people—our own people—who want to control our lives.

The spending is documented, the regulations are not temporary and the centralization of authority is camouflaged. True dangers are really with us and the trends seem to be unstoppable. Even though there is a growing outrage at drunken-sailor spending, government expansion and control is mounting, and a real fear is that the president, as commander-in-chief of the military, could use troops—not in foreign countries—but right here at home. The wars that ruined our image abroad and cost the nation billions of dollars (with no record of success) could become a problem right here at home. People are afraid to speak out in fear of being jailed without the right to habeas corpus.

Politicians who ride the government expansion think of themselves as heroes. Yet reality suggests that the government is making us less, not more secure, less, not more prosperous….and…. that government is less trusted than ever before. In effect, the central planning that began with 9-11 has become permanent as big government infringes on our freedom while it socializes and federalizes while giving us little but hassles in return.

The watchwords in Republican circles were once tied to private initiatives, the rights of the individual, private markets and private enterprise. Today, however the leviathan state is being challenged. And, while the forces of freedom may eventually prevail, the war on American values and ideals is being challenged by the very people that we have elected. Dissidents who challenge the omnipotent state face the possibility of jail. Plus—

Newpapers and electronic media are being duped by agency PR flaks who manipulate the news by planting stories and then having their bosses react to meet the purposes of either Congress or the Administration. It is a real mess...an exercise in dishonesty by those who govern. There are obvious governmental failures, however these are often, quite successfully, covered up. The power of lobbyists is sinful.

With conformation of government inadequacies all around us in the form of their doing nothing about soaring medical costs, skyrocketing national debt, inflation, out-of-control balance-of-payments, loss of liberties, and attacks on privileges granted by the Bill of Rights, one would think the populous would react. Yet, fear of reprisal is a common denominator for inaction because legislators follow the Mussolini principles of "nothing against the state."

To this I reply that under any form of state-ism, any individual or any intellectual must have the freedom to speak their mind and have a refuge from which to tell it without fear of incarceration.

Today, independent sectors-of-thought have never been more essential, yet, never have they been under so much pressure to be quiet. In the marketplace of ideas, it is time to re-invent the concepts of liberty.

-30-

Charlie Junior had read that article many times, and each time he read it he gleaned another jewel from its content. As both amateur historian and amateur soothsayer, CJ, especially without Alveta, wrestled with the past and with the future. In that regard, his concern was mainly what did Big Brother have in store for his children—little Alley, who was eleven; Katherine, seven and son Chuck. Photographs show that Chuck is a mirror image of his grandfather at the same age.

CJ felt quite alone at times and tear-time was often late at night after kneeling and reciting a special prayer to the Blessed Mother—the Memorie. When Alveta was alive, he had said this prayer in concert with her every morning as he pushed the covers off and knelt at bedside and she remained under the covers. The morning ritual was repeated every evening as their last action before going to sleep.

Tonight CJ, alone, repeated the words out loud and slowly:

Remember, oh most gracious Virgin Mary that never was it known that anyone who fled to thy protection, Implored your help, or sought your intersession was left unaided.

Inspired by this confidence I come to you, humbly and with profound love and gratitude, Oh Mother of the Word Incarnate, Please hear my petitions, and ask your son to answer them.   Amen

Charlie Junior had no petitions related to Alveta. He knew his wife had gone straight through the gates that Saint Peter was guarding. Alveta's love for him, and for Jesus, was really infinity to the infinity power.

Next he prayed, as he did frequently, for the men and women still serving in Iraq. The daily killings, the massacres, the kidnappings, the torture inflicted on those occupying the country was as awful today as it was 40 years ago just after President Bush had declared the war was won. "Won," he said to himself. "If this is winning a war, how does one lose?"

CHAPTER FOURTEEN
2072 – WHITE CLOAK LLC

Earlier in the year, Chuck had inherited total management responsibility for White Cloak LLC, a name shorter than before, a name meant to defuse references to paint, varnish and lacquer – especially lacquer. But, even with the name change, Chuck knew very well that he was a prime target for GEORGE's watch list, especially since GEORGE had taken over the FBI's national email monitoring tasks. Monitoring that did not require a court order.

With his dad's help, Chuck had streamlined production operations, added new reactors and mixing equipment and decreased employment from over one hundred people to less than forty. While publicly this decrease was tied to economics, in reality Chuck wanted to have only close personal friends working in the factory...people he could trust with his soul...people who were quiet...people who, on the surface were everyday folk, but whose hearts were bent on restoring personal individual freedoms to every citizen of the United States, born or naturalized.

Even then, only a few chosen employees really knew the underlying goals and mission of White Cloak. These goals were closely tied to a cadre of Americans across the country—about one dozen true states-rightsers who were trustworthy—who were truly concerned about personal invasion of privacy and were worried desperately about potential military action against private citizens. This concern was legitimate as exposed from leaked Pentagon memos as early as 2020. Military men in concert with hawk politicians, backed by businesses that were in line to profit handsomely, regardless of whether the country was being controlled by the radical right or the liberal left.

In this controlling effort, the communication media was often duped, often regurgitating government PR releases as if the news was fact. One really did not know what to believe in the press or on TV because leaks may be real or planted, true or untrue. Knowingly or unknowingly, many of the press supported the feds. In fact, many government officials became star press pawns; these officials thrived on media attention, and as "inside sources", these men and women often came back to use their planted stories to accomplish political goals. The press became pawns and puppets—often losing their credibility.

Every presidential administration since Ronald Reagan played footsies with the media, who, swear as they may to suggest independence, were puppets to both Republican and Democrat puppeteers. Then California Governor Arnold Swartzneger had been the most unusual media star while courting editors to back his bid for a constitutional amendment that would allow a foreigner to become president. Reason and the status quo prevailed in the long run. Also, Swartzneger lost his glamour when he goverened the state into bankruptcy.

Given the faulty, flagrant and falsified communication system, businessmen had to be careful when talking to editors or TV cameras and when visiting elected officials. With trepidation, Chuck interfaced with the press and with governmental bodies, especially state and federal environmental agencies. A student of history, Chuck had read how California governor Jerry Brown, Jr. would hold a press conference just before his agents would lead an entourage of editors and TV cameramen to a local refinery to descend on management and announce pollution fines. Weismantel did not want a press corps at his plant. Consequently, he was one of the few facilities in Houston to host periodic open houses for OSHA, EPA and the Texas Environmental Commission and editors, (as well as other acronymic agencies that were invited to these events).

If White Cloak was hiding something, it was not apparent because of the open door policy. Only Chuck and his dad, Charlie Junior, really knew the answer to what took place behind the walls of White Cloak. Five other devoted and trusted employees knew parts of the story of what took place behind closed doors. Charlie Junior and Chuck had arranged things so that none of his employees would ever have to lie.

CHAPTER FIFTEEN
2078 – CONFESSION

It had been a decade since his dad had taken him to The Point and told him the secrets behind White Cloak, LLC. Chuck had restructured the company as an LLC to avoid certain Texas Franchise Taxes, but later he incorporated in Nevada because only Nevada and Delaware had laws that truly had protective barriers for management and directors. Those business moves had nothing to do with the secrets at White Cloak LLC.

Chuck remembered that day on The Point; he remembered his dad examining the bass boat, he remembered the breakfast, he remembered the song of the black throated cardinal, and he remembered the confession...each word burned into his mind like a cowboy on the King Ranch branding the running W into the hide of a calf so that everyone will know exactly who owns this side of beef.

One decade ago, on that first day of confession at The Point, Charlie Junior had started the story, a three year story, with the words: "Son, it is time for you to know what you really own, and for you to understand its importance. The nation's freedom, at least what is left of it in these United States, may actually rest directly on your shoulders."

This seemed like much too awesome a statement for Charlie Junior to make, but as the story unfolded, the significance of what was iterated became astounding. His dad, and now he, was a part of an underground movement to assure democracy would always be there for everyone....and....not just available to a privileged few. Yet, it was an elite and privileged few that, despite rhetoric to the contrary, had managed to gain control of the government and the military in the United States. Controlling efforts were initiated *by The Omega Group*, which was the name his family had given to those who considered themselves puppeteers of the government and military – and – these two bodies were in the advent of controlling the country by taking away individual freedoms. Ironically, *The Omega Group* was leading the U.S. into a Saddam-Hussein-type government in our own country—a type of police-state that few recognized that was in its formation stage. The USA was beginning to emulate Iraq as Iraq was before the dictator's overthrow. This control by *The Omega Group* had started under Bush II and was exacerbated by the horrendous spending by Obama.

His dad's story—the story told at The Point—left Chuck flabbergasted. CJ had named names that were part of *Omega*.

It had been a lecture, a long lecture that divulged that his dad had surreptitiously become a patriarch of an underground power that would be given to his son. During this revelation, there was no room for questions, at least not during the dissertation. Questions would come later. There would be many questions because almost every minute Chuck would say to himself: Who? What? When? Where? Why? How? It was an incredible story that began in 1989 when his grandfather began to monitor an upstart little oil company by the name of Harken Energy. Harken was the premier financial funnel to George W. Bush, and its sister was Halliburton.

Looking back on that day in 2068 at The Point, Chuck had watched CJ stand up and begin pacing back and forth across the sand, first explaining the reason why The Point was chosen as the site for secret discussions. It turns out that his father, this simple, holy man, was, in fact, the mastermind of intrigue, a genius in electronic monitoring, acoustical data gathering, vibration monitoring, military G-2, explosives and munitions, aircraft, high-speed communications and spy satellites. In awe he learned that he himself was being monitored 24 hours a day, at home, at work, in his car...his Durango was bugged...and right then and there on The Point both of them were being viewed by satellite. CJ had made Chuck get his fishing pole so that they could sit beside one another so that the space monitor would believe that they were simply sitting there, innocently fishing. His dad spoke mainly when landing planes flew overhead because this noise muffled any acoustic surveillance from orbiting satellites.

Every one of Chuck's credit card transactions was being collected in a master databank. The system used to trace him, to track him, right here in the U.S. or anywhere in the world, was a state-of-the-art version of the monitoring system developed by DARPA to observe, record, and detect the action of terrorists or perceived terrorists in Iraq. Chuck, because he was CJ's son, was a perceived threat to those in control of *The Omega Group*. They even watched Chuck while he was in church.

Chuck was no dummy and was quite aware of the cloak and dagger operations that were going on. He had learned that ACXIOM, who has data on everyone, was interfacing with the government spy agencies and providing those agencies with detailed financial data on White Cloak including all purchases of every raw material. ACXIOM also had a complete personal dossier on Chuck. He knew this because he also had contacts with people in important places.

Chuck knew that his driving whereabouts were a daily record. Indeed, in 2007 every speed pass for every toll way across the nation had been integrated to monitor individual automobiles (in order to monitor the location of individual people). And in 2010 all cars, no matter where they were in the world, could be located by using an electronic transmission chip (embedded within the super glue that attaches the mirror to the windshield of each car or truck) as a satellite tracking device. And, if the chip was removed, authorities were immediately notified. While the story given to the public was that each vehicle being sold had this safety device to facilitate emergency help, it was really a DTC-sponsored legislation to help Big Brother watch you wherever you go.

There was virtually no safe haven, not even in your own home.

CHAPTER SIXTEEN
2078 – FISHING

They had been at The Point for two hours and CJ's story continued:

Sitting next to his dad, Chuck listened, listened, listened, and listened. Both of them would reel in, stand up and cast, and, fortunately, just to make things look legitimate, a fish would strike the bait and they would catch something. They were using the universal bait – hot dogs.

"Here is how it started, and here is why it started." That is how Charlie Junior began the story that had been hidden from Chuck until now.

"Mom and Dad, like me and like you, were professional chemical engineers. More importantly, they had an uncanny insight in respect to what was going on around them. Perhaps their twenty-two year age difference gave them a two-generation perspective on life that most couples didn't have.

"Anyway, as early as the presidential days of Ronald Reagan, my dad, who always voted as a conservative, he was a Goldwater backer, saw the evolution of the Republican party as one that no longer believed in fiscal conservation or small government. Reagan spent money faster than a Democrat.....and....under Reagan...legislation made its way through Congress benefiting a paltry few at the top of the business hill. Always included with this elite was *The Omega Group*, cozying up to whomever was in the White House.

"Reagan, for example, spent billions to reward hawks and the pro-military. This was a giant step in giving unruly power to a few people. Those people, married to lies that Iraq had weapons of mass destruction, would eventually send the nation into war with Iraq without regard to the consequences. The Bush dynasty—virtually controlled by six *Omega* partners—two in The White House and four in the Pentagon—had unbridled power. Very few people knew that the dynasty was beholden to Rockefeller money which is what sent the Bush family from Maine trekking to Texas in the first place.

"But, it was Reagan who started the deficit spending by printing more money than newspaper. It was he who adopted a spend,

spend, spend policy and promoted liaise faire into sinfulness. One Northern California company, Pacific Lumber, was hit by corporate raiders who bought the company with a loan from investment bankers tied to *Omega*. Then, after the acquisition was completed, the new owners raided the company's retirement fund using the money to pay off the loan. It was an absolute sham, but Reagan's White House didn't raise an eyebrow. Later, Bush-II stood inactively by as the entire Pacific Lumber plant—the whole operation—was closed in 2009.

"This kind of chicanery continued, under both Republicans and Democrats, with Republicans always forcing more into the military budget, and with both parties bowing to *Omega*. NAFTA turned out to be the crowning blow. Unions, at least the unions who manufactured 'things' had called the shots correctly in predicting that high paying manufacturing jobs would be sent overseas. In the USA, automation was not a panacea. Why? Because it takes only a Rhode Island minute to understand that it doesn't take a thirty dollar per hour person to watch a robot weld an auto hood. That welding could take place in front of a four dollar worker in Mexico, which brings us back to NAFTA. I remember this story so well.

"Dad got the complete proposal for NAFTA. It was a stack of papers at least two feet high. He and Mom meticulously went through every page trying to find out why so many *Omega* players were solidly behind it.   At the time NAFTA had not passed, and when Dad got to the section on banking and finance he found out why. That part of NAFTA was running into trouble in Mexico.

"Mom quizzed him relentlessly about this section of NAFTA and he was emphatic saying: 'I guarantee you, as soon as the banks and money people get what they want, NAFTA will pass easily.'

"Resistance to NAFTA, and particularly to that section of the agreement was heated and severely criticized by a key Mexican Presidential candidate and a Catholic Bishop. Both of them were murdered over a period of months. With this opposition out of the way, the banking section passed in all three countries and soon after NAFTA became law, despite union ranting.   From that point on unions became virtually powerless. The situation was exacerbated by the quantum jump of economic power in China.

"During this time Mom and Dad pinpointed the Ivy League connection to *Omega* and also to key politicians in Mexico. In particular, Harvard and Yale money became very active, often backing corporate raiders. Large pharmaceutical companies amassed fortunes by gouging people for medication, and cartels, like vegetable oil companies, held secret meetings to divide up the world into market shares that led to monopolize prices. Some of these guys were caught, but fines were only a slap on the wrist. In fact, the culprits were rewarded with large biodiesel subsidies.

"Later, there was a financial catastrophe in the sub-prime mortgage industry, and that was preceded by subversion in the mutual fund derrivative industry which was rocked with scandal.

"Even the most venerable woman of all, Martha Stewart, was convicted for having her hand in the cookie jar. Energy companies, one was called Enron, collapsed under the pressure of accounting fraud. By 2008, crude oil reached

$145 per barrel and natural gas prices sky-rocketed to fives times their value. When natural gas users turned to LNG, liquefied natural gas, the power industry, who had spent billions to use natural gas to produce electricity turned their attention back to coal and nuclear. Billions of dollars changed hands in the process. And, through it all, *Omega* took its share and never lost a penny."

After an hour of listening, Chuck interjected two words: "About *Omega*?" His dad interrupted him: "I'll tell you more about *Omega*, but first you have to understand what prompted the Weismantels to form White Cloak Paint, Varnish & Lacquer."

He continued: "My dad believed that for *Omega* to truly rule the country and in order to avoid anarchy, they had to control the military. To do this, all they had to do was control the presidency, and that could be done by controlling the Congressional precincts, by buying certain politicians, and manipulating the media and the communications industry.

"FTC rulings allowed monopolies to exist and that control started right here in Texas when an upstart San Antonio company called

Clear Channel started buying up hundreds of radio stations. George-Bush-the-Junior was governor at the time and he paved the way for such acquisitions by stacking the Public Utility Commission with people who would vote pro-*Omega* even when they didn't know *The Omega Group* existed. Their rewards were positions and power in the administration, first in Texas and eventually in DC.

"Next, using the Kennedy era and Reagan years as precedent, Congress abrogated their constitutional responsibility regarding the right to declare war, and, the next thing you know Bush-Number-Two invaded Iraq and unbelievably, we still have a large presence their today. Of course, that war was supposedly fought to combat terrorism and find weapons of mass destruction...but...none were found.

"Was that war really all about oil?" .... Yes!

"But, in the name of response to 9-11 and in the name of combating terrorism, the U.S. developed a military regime that is second only to China, and it was costing billions of dollars. That is what worried your grandfather. He

110

believed, as do I, that we, the citizens, are eventually going to be attacked by our own troops on our own soil. Khrushchev gets his way."

"What does that mean?" Chuck inquired.

"I'll explain," CJ said, "My comment was supposed to be a funny."

There was a long pause, and Charlie Junior continued the revelation to his son, and Chuck was assimilating his dad's words as quickly as he could, never fathoming what he would hear next. He was hardly getting a chance to ask a question.

"Son, what you don't know is White Cloak has secretly been manufacturing millions of pounds of explosives, using a TNT base, in preparation for the people to fend off an attack by our own armed forces. You own an ammunition plant and an arsenal. That arsenal is secretly stashed in seven sites across the U.S., and the amount is larger than all the black powder duPont made during the Civil War."

Precisely as Charlie Junior put a period on that sentence, his reel began to spin out of control and, even though the drag was set tightly, this fish was winning the battle, if it was a fish. It was almost like CJ had hooked onto a log.

Charlie Junior thought he had hooked a hundred pound gar, and because their reels were wound with eight pound monofilament, he had little hope of catching this monster.

But, after almost an hour, the fish lay exhausted on the sand bar just below the water surface, Chuck waded into water and jammed a large stainless steel treble hook into the catfish's mouth. The fish was so worn out that he didn't even flinch. He weighed 36 pounds if he weighed an ounce. The treble hook was attached to a three-foot rope that Chuck always carried, hoping for just such an occasion. They hauled him in.

"Fish fry!" CJ hollered.

"You bet," Chuck chimed.

"For a brief moment, time stopped, government power was forgotten, and Charlie Junior looked at Chuck: "There is a lot more to tell you, son."

Chuck said: "I can imagine, but where? When?"

"There are bugs everywhere," Charlie Junior said. "There are only a couple other safe communication spots. The Point is one of them. I'll explain later. Right now let's go fillet a catfish."

CHAPTER SEVENTEEN
2078 – A NEW DRIVER

Once Chuck understood that he was actually the owner of a paint factory that was really a munitions factory that was producing explosives to protect the people from its own army, he was dazed. He had a million more questions, and, as he walked through the plant the following day, he asked: "How was all of this going on right under my nose?"

Bobby Atkins was standing over a large tank that utilized an old 100 horsepower Mooney disperser. Bobby was tossing in bags of titanium dioxide, the white pigment that is used in almost everything from rubber, to paint, to plastic, to toothpaste. Bobby saw Chuck coming toward him and waved, not saying anything because the roar of the U.S. Motor, a rarity these days with all of the motors coming in from China, was drowning out his voice.

Chuck returned the greeting with a thumbs up, and continued walking past the ball mills, the sand mills, past the roller mills and the old stone mill. The old stone mill had originally been used to make Morehouse Mustard; the old roller mill had originally been used to make

Ghirardelli Chocolate in San Francisco. That whole chocolate complex is now a tourist spot called Ghirardelli Square and the chocolate comes from......who knows where?

Chuck walked past the reactors and paid particular attention to Reactor "K". He never had known why there was a reflux condenser to catch escaping solvent on the top of that unit. Now he knew why. He found his dad way out back near the property line where there were three open-fire varnish kettles. All three kettles were cooking, and each was tied to a portable condenser that collected all forms of air pollution from volatile organics to fine particulates.

Charlie Junior was talking to A-J Brown, a varnish maker about the same age as his dad; although neither of them looked to be 82, neither did they act that age. Chuck motioned to his dad to come over and Chuck handed him a note. They didn't speak because of the roar of the open fires that were blasting two-foot long blue and yellow flames against the bottom of the kettles. The note said: "Tonight at The Point at six o'clock."

CJ gave him a thumbs up and took a pen from his overalls and wrote on the same note: "I'll pick you at 5:30 PM; let's use the Mustang." Chuck gave his dad a thumbs up. Then, took the note and threw it into the open fire where it succumbed to the flames that changed the ink-on-cellulose to carbon dioxide. Chuck said to himself: "I have just contributed to global warming."

Camouflaged in fishing gear, they reached The Point at 6:00 PM as planned. They wore long sleeves but the mosquitoes were bad that evening so they took turns spraying one another with Off and CJ said: "Don't forget behind the ears and the hands and fingers." He also sprayed the outside of his pants legs commenting: "These skeeters are vicious."

Chuck said: "Did you ever hear the story of the Texas skeeter? Chuck told it and Charlie Junior laughed, but deep down he really didn't think the joke was funny.

"Dad," Chuck said, "Do I have to learn to make Super-Sol?" Super-Sol was the secret name for the incendiary manufactured at White Cloak.

That was a funny question, but it was a serious question and it had serious consequences. CJ did not take the question lightly.

"I'm 82 years old," he said. "I feel like I'm 62, but we all know that I've brought my net worth to zero and it is a matter of time." He looked serious.

"Yes, son, you should understand Super-Sol, but more importantly, you have to know and understand the big plan and must be able to interface with the total team. Parks and Woodbury both have sons that are involved." Parks and Woodberry were two of Charlie Junior's closest friends who lived in Pecos and Cold Springs, Texas, respectively.

"I have been trying to figure out my exit strategy and I think it is tied to music," Charlie Junior said.

"What?" Chuck looked surprised.

"Here is the plan; it is one that allows us to meet, somewhat inconspicuously at my house even though we know we will be monitored."

"Also," he said, "do you remember the sign language that Mrs. Buckstaff taught you in the sixth grade so that you could communicate with deaf people?"

"Sure," he replied.

"Good—here is what we'll do."

CHAPTER EIGHTEEN
2078 – MUTE

With Chuck knowing only part of the story, Charlie Junior had to search for an early opportunity to tell Chuck "the rest of the story." When that thought went through his brain, Charlie Junior mentally reminisced "I wonder what ever happened to Paul Harvey?"

So on Tuesday of the same week – the same week that Chuck had learned about munitions – Chuck would also learn how to make "Super-Sol" – the code name for an explosive that may be needed in the future to arm the people against the military. CJ entered Chuck's office and slipped a note in front of his son. It said: "I will meet you in the lobby of the courthouse in Cold Springs at exactly 10:10 AM today. Wear you hiking boots." It was 9:00 AM. Then he continued: "Remember, we are always being watched, and the Durango is bugged. The Mustang is the only safe car."

Chuck winked at his dad but did not utter a word. Charlie Junior put the note in his mouth and left the office stopping in the men's room and flushing the note down the commode knowing full well that even the sewage generated at White Cloak was being monitored. Chuck went to the front door that exits to the plant parking lot. He stopped to tell his secretary: "Sue, can you cancel my afternoon appointments, please. Something has come up."

Sue was a pretty little woman; she had worked at White Cloak since she was nineteen. The company paid her way through business school and she was the only person in the whole organization who had single signature signing authority on company checks. That is how much she was trusted. She had worked side by side with his dad since before Alveta died. Chuck asked himself: "How much does she know?" Perhaps he would know that answer to that question a little after 10:10 AM today.

As Chuck started out the factory door, he stopped, walked back into his office and placed his cell phone inside the roll top desk that he loved so much. That turned out to be a smart thing to do. For, as he would learn later, not only was his phone bugged, but also its broadcast wavelengths were monitored 100% of the time.

Chuck had just enough time to get a haircut and drive to Cold Springs where he arrived at 10:01 AM.

He could see that his dad had already arrived because the Mustang was there on the West side of the courthouse building under a big live oak. There was a policeman standing in front of the 'stang, and Chuck wondered aloud: "What's that all about?"
He walked up the nine steps to the first floor of the courthouse building and there was his dad, in the hallway, talking to a man who looked a bit younger than his father. Charlie Junior waved him over and as Chuck neared the two seniors, CJ spoke: "Chuck, I'd like you to meet Judge Woodbury...Sam, I'd like you to meet my son, Chuck."

Woodbury responded: "Glad to meet you son, I know both of your sisters."

Chuck thought that mentioning his sisters was unusual, but said nothing about it. Looking the judge straight in the eye and firmly squeezing his hand, Chuck said: "I'm very glad to meet you sir."

Sir and m'am were common courtesies embedded in both Texas and Weismantel language and tradition. Before Chuck could respond to any other question or ask one of his own, CJ spoke: "See you later Sam; I have to take Chuck down to Double Lake to look at a paint job. Besides, Pete is probably tired of watching my car."

After goodbyes in the hallway, the two Weismantels headed out the West door where Charlie Junior hailed Pete, the officer standing next to the Mustang. "Thanks, Pete." His dad headed directly to the trunk and opened it pulling out a one pound box of Martha Washington chocolates. He gave them to Pete saying: "Be sure to share these with the girls."

Pete smiled a thank you.

CJ said: "I'll drive," and son and father fell into the bucket seats before backing up and sending the black beauty back down FM 2025 toward Cleveland, with Double Lake approaching on the left.

"How do you know Woodbury?" Chuck asked. But, before his dad could answer, he asked a second question: "Is it safe?" He meant is it safe to talk.

"Yes," his Dad answered, and, "I've known Woodbury for years – ever since I worked on that produced water problem out in Mentone above Pecos." Chuck knew that project well. His dad had been asked to address the problem of radioactive isotopes in the water coming up with the oil out of the Delaware Basin reservoir. His dad had been waist deep in legal action for several years.

The subject changed: "What was Pete doing to your car?"

"Watchin' it," Charles said. "It's SOP whenever I visit the judge. The Mustang is monitored 24 hours a day so that it never can be bugged." He paused. "Are you wearing your boots?"

"Sure am," Chuck assured.

They turned left into Double Lake, took the starboard fork in the road and drove five thousand two hundred and eighty feet to the little store near the boat house. No one was there this time of year. Then, his dad did a crazy loop in order to drive down a somewhat secret path that dead-ended at an old log cabin that, in fact, was a log cabin garage. By manipulating a series of wires and weights, the garage door opened.

The door, and the width of the garage, was just wide enough for the driver to get out. So, CJ got out of the Ford and Chuck drove the vehicle inside the cabin. Before they left the car there, sealed shut with no possible entry, CJ reached for his keys and hit the button that popped open the trunk. There was a backpack and two shoulder canteens. "I brought some goodies and agua," he said. Chuck shouldered the pack; each took a canteen, and they began to trudge one mile to the circle.

There was a chill in the February air so both men donned their jackets and Chuck questioned: "Where to?"

"We'll head North for about a mile up the Sam Houston Trail, then hike up to the Forest Ranger's Circle. No one will be there."

Chuck knew the route well. He and his two sisters had often hiked it with Charlie Junior and Alveta. He could remember at least one of those first escapades when he was in the backpack.

The path was in pretty bad shape because it had not been traveled much during the winter. The path jumped from one side of a creek to the other, back and forth, and, in some places, the creek bed was a deep ditch dropping 14 feet below the hikers. Trees had fallen, probably during one of the big rainstorms the area had experienced in the late fall of '77, and trunks blocked the path requiring the men to trek around large branches and through blackberry bushes about to sprout. The thorns snagged their pants. This was mainly CJ's problem because he had on a sweat suit; Chuck had jeans.

They arrived at the circle about 12:30 PM. Charlie Junior pulled out his canteen and stood there, sipping slowly, before sitting on one of the logs that were arranged theatre-style-in-the-round. Chuck remembered being there as a kid listening to the ranger tell the mysteries of this state forest preserve that was part of The Big Thicket. There were over one hundred different species of trees within a half-mile radius of right where he was standing.

His dad began: "Woodbury is the leader." He said it cryptically, hoping Chuck would question him, and Chuck did:

"Leader?" Chuck asked.

"Yes," Charlie Junior answered with emphasis: "Leader."

"When I was in Pecos running between there, Midland and Monahan, that's when I met Joe Parks – Judge Joe Parks." Almost as a sidebar he added: "I knew the instant that I shook his hand, he was a True Texan."

Those two words—True Texan—were words that Chuck had heard all his life. A True Texan meant more than being a person who says yes sir and yes m'am; it was more than tipping ten gallons to a lady, it was more than knowing how to saddle a horse or squeeze a man's hand as you looked him straight in the eye. It meant more than being born Texan. Being a True Texan meant that you never have to question a man's word, you never needed a piece of paper for there to be a contract, and it meant that if you gave this person your soul for two years that they would give it back to you in better shape than if you had kept it yourself.

If Parks was a True Texan, Chuck knew what it meant. It did not mean a carpetbagger from Maine.

CJ challenged Chuck to recall their first discussion at The Point.

"Do you remember our Part One discussion at The Point?"

Chuck nodded his head.

"Well, this is Part Two." He reached over and picked up a large fully opened pine cone and began to peel off the seeds one by one. "We are way out here in the Thicket because it is one of the few places GEORGE can't find us."

He continued after throwing the cone into the woods, and, then he sat, resting his rear on one of the log seats.

"Son," he began, "this story begins with your grandparents, but, the story really begins to unfold when your grandmother died. One of her last wishes was in the form of a promise elicited from me, was that I would continue to try to do something to restore freedom to the individual here in the United States. She was almost paranoid about what was happening to people in respect to government intervention in a person's daily life. As a result of her prying, our family has forever been suspect by federal investigators and from all acronyms involved with security.

"Our personal lives are well documented in records in DC, and we know that that intervention has become more excessive as I

127

have grown older, even as you have grown older. And, as I have said before, your grandparents saw it coming.

"For a chemical engineer to be worried about the country's freedom seemed like a monumental task—but—at her request—a request coming from someone who, politically, never even had the desire to even be on a school board—I took her request seriously. Your grandmother was special, and she passed her dedication and her fears to your mother. Even though your mom was just a child, these two women had empathy despite their age difference. Somehow I think your grandmother knew that your mom and I would someday be together.

"Right after we were married—." He stopped right in the middle of the sentence and lamented: "God I wish she was here…only 36." CJ meant that Alveta was only 36 when she died. Chuck knew that.

"What you don't know, Chuck," his dad continued, is that I have always suspected foul play in her death."

Chuck sat up straight. This was something that hit him like a jolt of 480-volt power. "What??" he said.

"Chuck, your mom and I, especially your mom, were digging deeply into who makes up *The Omega Group*. She was deeply involved in a Pelican-Brief-type investigation. It was unilateral but the idea came from Parks and Woodbury who had evidence that key army bases in Texas, Kansas, Louisiana, and Georgia had generals who were thinking coupe ...coupe not in the normal sense.... but with generals in concert with certain politicians and, under The Patriot Act, would take out large segments of the population who they felt had questionable allegiance."

"Take out, as in **t-a-k-e-o-u-t**," CJ spelled out each letter, and added: "as in 'kill'." Chuck look flabbergasted.

"Yes, and in large numbers. Under cloak-and-dagger conditions disguising themselves as a legitimate business with ties to Israel, GEORGE approached two New York public relations firms who normally do political work, and asked them if they could develop a PR program that would focus on making black

Americans with Islamic-sounding names begin to look bad in the news, magazine articles and other media.

"Your mom was an expert, a genius in PR and she got wind of it through some of her international contacts. She began to snoop; we are sure GEORGE learned about her interest. Two weeks later she was vomiting, experiencing dehydration and she never recovered from, what now we believe was a poison called coderacim. As you know, neither Mom nor I wanted to be kept alive by extraordinary means, and, she died and was cremated even before my head was on straight. Of course, if we had done a CSI-Miami-type autopsy, the police report would not have given me true results anyway, so, the question of her being poisoned became moot.

"Woodbury was the one that uncovered a file on Mom. He has friendly contacts inside the Pentagon. The file indicated that she was getting dangerously close to information that key people did not want her to have in her possession—in fact—they did not want anyone to have the information. Before she died, Alveta at least knew I had mobilized, or at least was

130

trying to put into place, a resistance effort to combat the attacks we expect."

"You're not talking terrorists attacks are you?"

"No, I'm talking about attacks on U.S. citizens by U.S. soldiers all in the name of anti-terrorism. The seed of this idea for such powers was planted in 2004 when certain individuals, high up in the Pentagon, and tied to a team of players loyal to Donald Rumsfeld, Secretary of Defense, suggested to President Bush that he consider a long-term strategy to combat Islam here at home by isolation, and, if necessary, brute force. Arrests and torture were part of the plan...a plan blessed, unbelievably, by Bush's attorney generals."

"Is that when the Immigration and Naturalization Service virtually stopped issuing visas to people from that part of the world?"

"No, that was much later, but one thing I remember clearly – Charles and Cathy Weismantel – your grandparents—staunch Republicans all their lives – voted for a Democrat to be president. It was dad's opinion that his party had abandoned him and had abandoned basic conservative philosophies. He called Bush an FDR Democrat."

CJ stood up and started walking in a circle within the forest-ranger's circle that was about ten feet in diameter, stirring up dust, kicking pine cones and mumbling. He might have been praying, Chuck thought. After three loops, Chuck said:

"Dad?"

And with unusual empathy, repeated: "Dad, are you okay?"

Charlie Junior looked at his son, walked to him and hugged him.

"Parks, Woodbury, and I met in Pecos two weeks later. I remember the dinner vividly. I pulled the Mustang out of the garage at one in the morning and drove in circles and in back tracks for over two hours before placing the hammer down on a beeline for Pecos. No one knew where I was. Everyone thought I had taken off for Costa Rica to spend time getting through the depression of losing my wife. I had mentioned that Central American trek to Sue, who, at the time was a cute little, wet-behind-the-ears twenty-some year old who had just joined the company. I will tell you more about

Sue. She is a key part of our organization, but don't let me digress.

"The day I got there, to Pecos, that evening, Joe and I and Clint Yaeger, and a cowboy named Sparks, ordered four porterhouse steaks very rare. We were back in a dark corner of little hole-in-the-wall restaurant called Nellie's North without one drop of booze in our system.

"Cogent? Yes we were; we had to be. We were planning on how to defend ourselves from—against—the U.S. Army and U.S. Marines. It was really the president that we were afraid of because, ever since Bush II, the following administrations seem to have a free-hand in troop control. After all, the presidential position does include the job of being commander-in-chief, which, I might add is quite ironic because the U.S. was so adamant that the president of Pakistan should not carry both of those titles. But, but that is another story.....of how we got crossways with Pakistan.

"Parks knew that if citizens were going to have to fight the U.S. Army and Marines, there would need a very explosive liquid, lots of it, and we needed a place to manufacture and store thousands—maybe millions of gallons."

Chuck's face wrinkled: "I don't understand."

"Yes," CJ said, "I'm going too fast and I'm leaving out essential parts of the story.

"To begin with, just about the time you were born, we had enough evidence to be sure that a military takeover was being planned by *Omega* people planted in the Pentagon. The idea was not to put a general in place of the president, but – backed by *The Omega Group* — to assure there was a general who was actually controlling the president. This was kind-of-like what Dick Cheney did when George Bush was president -- and twenty years ago when the latest Kennedy was president and his cousin was White House Chief of Staff.

Charlie Junior stopped....and......he spit..........and.......he said: "Paternalism in the United States stinks." Then he went on............

"Given White Cloak's access to nitrocellulose, acetates, ketones, sulfur saltpeter, activated carbon and nitrogen, I developed a very stable explosive with an unlimited shelf life that has the power of tri-nitro-toluene and the pourability of napalm. I wanted to call it Fruit Juice, but seeing drums of Fruit Juice in a paint plant did not make sense. Mom came-up with the name Super-Sol and we even have a brochure about the product, showing it as a down-hole, biologically-safe polyol used for enhanced oil recovery. If someone orders it, we send them biodiesel fuel—the same biodiesel fuel that we use in our boilers. That way nothing is traceable."

"You mean Super-Sol in NOT Super-Sol?"

"That's what I mean," Charlie Junior said.

"And, we needed a place to store all this stuff we were making, so that's why we called it a specialty product for the oil patch. There are hundreds of old oil wells with Super-Sol tanks on site. The wells have been plugged and abandoned for years. Parks and his West Texas cowboys have been filling these tanks with Super-Sol. The location chain of these tanks extends two hundred miles, and if they ever begin to blow, half of the Permian Basin would end up West of Santa Fe and East of Shreveport.

"All these years, I have worked late on Tuesday and Thursday. Why? Do you know the Number K reactor? The 500 gallon reactor use to make automotive lacquers?"

"Yes."

"On those nights when I work late, Bobby Atkins and I are manufacturing explosives in Reactor K."

"Bobby Atkins?" Chuck queried, "All these years?"

"Yes, son, Bobby Atkins and three others in the plant have held this secret for over two decades. In the office, Sue knows everything. It is her accounting powers that have enabled us to hide the Super-Sol production."

"How?"

"All the paint and coatings and regular lacquer batches are designed for 103 gallon yield or 1030 for the large volume batches. Standard practice includes a 3% loss in transfer lines, fill lines, tanks and other units. But, we are meticulous in purging those lines with gaseous nitrogen to clean them and eliminate that yield loss. The nitrocellulose that is really NOT lost," he emphasized the word NOT lost, "ends up as Super-Sol."

"So that is why there has been a ten drum order of Super-Sol going to Pecos, Texas every week for all these years?"

"Yes, son."....."We've been preparing for war."

CHAPTER NINETEEN
1989 – ALAN ZUDIS

When the motor burned out in the clothes dryer, Charles had dismantled the appliance into all its component parts and determined that it was cheaper to buy a new one rather than to repair this old albatross.   For the moment, despite being against the rules of the deed restriction committee, he decided to hang a clothesline between two of the 50 pine trees in the backyard, saying to himself: "If I put it in the right place, no one will see it."

What Charles did not anticipate was that Cathy would have to go to four different stores to find a clothesline and clothes pins. She had to settle for spring-loaded because no one seemed to make the single-split-shaft pins anymore—the kind made out of one piece of wood and which used camming action to hold the pin to the clothes and to the line.

After installing the line two days ago, the rain came. The clothesline drooped and thus required pulling it taut again, and again. Maintaining tension would require constant attention until the new dryer was purchased…a purchase that did not come quickly for reason and after reason.

This Easter Sunday morning found Charles in front of the clothesline. Holy Saturday evening he had hung out the washing. Now he was feeling both the bath and hand towels and socks for dampness. Making the decision they were dry enough to de-pin, he took them inside.

He threw the largest towels over his shoulder first, then the smaller ones and finally each individual sock found their way to his left shoulder where the stack of dry clothes, well, virtually dry, reached ear level, with his socks riding on top of the pile.

With the equivalent of two laundry loads clinging precariously to his shoulders, Charles entered the back utility room door, turned sideways to allow himself in, and then he turned sideways again—in a reverse direction— maneuvering the stack of clothes on his shoulder so that he could enter into the kitchen.

As he made his way inside, laundry still on his shoulder, he reached into the microwave to retrieve a cup of "nuked" coffee before ascending to the second floor. Halfway up the stairs, he noticed that the top sock – the white one with a gray heel and a golden toe – was slipping from its precarious perch, and before one might say "Jack Robinson" the gravitational pull on that single sock forced it down where it landed—bulls eye—in the cup of hot, black coffee. He stopped....looked at the comedy taking place at his expense....and proceeded up the stairs, through the master bedroom and into the bathroom, where, Cathy was brushing her teeth.

"Princess," he said. Princess was a pet name, and one that Cathy cherished. He continued, "May I get to the sink?"

As he said this, she backed away while the battery operated tooth brush buzzed as Charles placed the cup, filled with an athletic sock acting as a coffee wick, into the sink.

She turned off the brush; she stood there; she looked at him as toothpaste drool wept down the side of her lips; her eyes said: "What is this all about?"

He shrugged his shoulders and returned to the bedroom, throwing the rest of the laundry onto the California-king-size bed. He sat down while saying: "Rule Number One: the absorbency of one thick athletic sock is approximately equal to one cup of coffee!"

They laughed, she in the bathroom, and he flopping down onto the bed lying on his back. He heard her rinse her mouth and then a thump, thump, thump as her heels hit the floor running into the bedroom and flinging herself on top of him. Her action took him totally by surprise, and as she lay on top of him smothering him with kiss after kiss after kiss, while still in her all-together, she stopped, looked into his eyes and, while caressing his ear, demurely whispered: "I enjoy being a girl."

Yet, immediately, she proved she was a woman.

That evening, after the children were in bed, Charles and Cathy stood together in the kitchen. She was washing and he was drying the dishes. He leaned over her shoulder as she stood facing the sink and quietly put his lips close to her ear saying, "Thank you for this afternoon. Happy Easter."

She giggled and replied, "Oh, it was just a case of spontaneous combustion."

"Indeed!" he said. "Indeed."

And soon they were back in bed. This time the fire burned more slowly, but always lovingly.

Charles looked at his beautiful, young wife and said, "The love you have inside of you is so powerful that a man would be an idiot not to want that love directed squarely toward him and to try—in every way possible—to return the favor of this blessing."

"And you do," Cathy replied with love in her heart and in her eyes.

Monday morning Charles rose early, walked three miles, came home, showered and was about to head off to work as Cathy, sleepy-eyed, got her first glimpse of the cup of coffee (French roast) that he had placed next to her on the night stand as he woke her by kissing her goodbye.

She said, "Where are you going so early?" It was six minutes after six.

"I have a breakfast meeting with Al Zudis," Charles said, adding, "You know he likes to get an early start."

Cathy frowned a bit, Charles saw it...the frown...but he didn't say anything.

She <u>did</u> say something.

"Don't you think it is a waste of your time meeting with Al?"

Charles said, "You could be right, but I must see this through. I may not have many more opportunities to talk to him." Alan Zudis was 92 years old. "I'll tell you all about it this afternoon."

He blew her a kiss.

He stopped.

Caught in the act of not showing his true love for her, he amended his route, returned to the bedside, sat down, leaned over, kissed Cathy on the forehead, on her nose, each cheek and softly on her lips, and said two words twice.

"Always princess. Always princess."

In a moment he was gone from the room, engaged in the 30 mile trip to Denny's on 225 in Pasadena, Texas, a place Charles jokingly called his ship channel office. Like Jack London had his favorite hangout, this breakfast joint was Charles' First and Last Chance Saloon.

Charles walked into Denny's and looking left into the smoking section, he saw Alan Zudis was already there drinking coffee, already smoking, already schmoozing up to the waitress. "Why?" Charles said to himself. "Why does he always beat me here?" What Charles never knew or never would know is that this Denny's was also the Zudis' hangout each morning where Alan would spend hours reading oil exploration and production periodicals and the daily *Financial Times*.

Over here, Zudis motioned, and, as Charles moseyed toward the table for six, which was filled with magazines and papers, Noel the waitress questioned: "Black coffee, Mr. W?"

"Yes m'am," he replied, followed by, "Hi Al."

Alan Zudis was 44 years his senior, and Alan had lived through the glory years of Houston, the boom years in oil, and the recent bust. Alan knew everyone, all the early wildcatters like Glen McCarthy and Michael Halbouty, George Strake and other key players in the industry, like George R. Brown, Red Adair and Available Jones. He knew politicians, and city fathers and city mothers. For example, he had been a strong supporter of Estelle Hobby when she was instrumental in forming the Woman's Army Corp under FDR at Ellington Field during the Second World War.

Zudis had not gone off to war because he was instrumental to the oil and gas needs of the military. He knew all the ways to get energy out of the ground at a time when fuel was vital for jeeps, tanks, and planes. Charles sat down across from this energy genius, a conservative Democrat by choice but a conservative Republican by 1989 standards.

"Hi Charles," Al responded. "Did you have any trouble finding the place?"

They both laughed because they both knew they had been meeting there for many years.

"Not a problem," Charles replied. "The Broadway exit still works." He smiled. "My treat this morning," meaning he would pop for breakfast.

To this Zudis replied, "Good. I didn't bring any money anyway." He stopped, threw a slick in front of Charles and said, "Look at this." Charles picked up the magazine. It was the March issue of *World Energy / Oil & Gas* and saw the cover story "Harken Heating Up."

Charles knew all about Harken. A friend of his worked at Harken and had been filling him on the Bush connections to Harken and how Harvard money and influence was making this piddley little company into a multi-billion dollar enterprise because Bush Senior made sure that his son was getting concessions for Middle East oil drilling in the "sure-thing" producing area in the Southern Mediterranean. Harken was in the middle of a boom. This pretty much proved that their management and key players held the kind of positions that would favor contact with *The Omega Group*. The people at Harken's top were going to make big money before the little investors would get in and lose a bundle.

"This looks like stuff for throne reading," Charles said as he placed the publication aside. Zudis nodded his head adding, "You know he's a carpetbagger, don't you?"

With that statement, Zudis had thrown Charles a curve ball, and Charles would be swinging blindly unless he 'fessed up that he didn't have notion of what Zudis was talking about.

"I think you lost me, Al." Charles had a question mark all over his face and in the inflection of his voice. Zudis was ready to dive in with an explanation. He said, "You don't think coming down here to Texas was Bush's idea do you?" He paused. "God knows it was

Rockefeller and his cronies' idea to send him here and put him into business in the middle of the oil patch."

Alan paused for breath and then continued. "They knew that as our resources petered out it would eventually drive up the price of oil and natural gas. Nelson and all of *The Omega Group* would get in low and sell high......and higher......and higher. Bet my word that someday all the Seven Sisters will be back together again." Zudis was referring to the 1940s breakup of Standard Oil's seven components under anti-trust pressure. Zudis believed acquisitions and mergers would eventually put control of the U.S. energy market into the hands of a selected few.....to include institutions backed by sovereign funds. *The Omega Group* was referenced to the key investors who controlled all U.S. commodity markets, including oil and gas, grain, pharmaceuticals, metals and money.......yes... money is sometimes considered a commodity.

Zudis added, "None of us ol' timers ever trusted Fitzbush." This was his Texan way of referring to a Fitzpatrick, Fitzgerald, or a Fitzsimmons, where Fitz means "Bastard of."

Charles nodded and picked up the menu briefly, while at the same time looking for Noel. She spotted his glances and walked over to the table. "You need something Mr. W?"

"Yes," he said. "Don't you have an Original Grand Slam for a buck ninety nine?" She laughed flirtingly, and with a heavy Southern African-American accent said, "You're tellin' your age Mr. W. That price is as old as Methuselah."

She referred him to the fine print. There was the Original Slam that Charles ordered with eggs basted. It was now $2.99.

Zudis and Weismantel then proceeded to bury their heads together. They knew that video recorders monitored their every movement but felt quite safe in discussing confidential information about Zudis' new technology related to principles of gas lift pumping. His was a new way to economically recover natural gas in marginal fields. Charles hoped to apply this principle to the Texaco reserves near Pecos, Texas where the highly vicious, highly paraffinic waxed oils quickly clogged the pores of the production formations.

Both he and Zudis wanted to keep this technology somewhat secret and out of the hands of companies like Harken who—if they learned the technique and duplicated the equipment—would place it in the hands of the ARAMCOs of the world, who at some time in the future would reap financial benefits for *The Omega Group*, perhaps at the expense of the dollar, perhaps at the expense of the little American.

Both Charles and Al knew that *Omega* was eying the Middle East as an income source, and Iraq was high on the hit list.

CHAPTER TWENTY
2004 – LATE APRIL

"Well now, what are you going to do with it?"

"I don't know," Charles told Cathy.

They were looking at a very large piece of process equipment, a 200 hundred gallon tank with a jacketed heater around it and on the top was a 15 horsepower Lightening Mixer whose shaft angled directly into the vessel at a 30° angle.

"As it now stands, it wouldn't have worked anyway because it is not totally sealed at the top." Both chemical engineers nodded their heads in agreement.

This equipment was just part of a Super Critical Water Oxidization (SCWO) unit that Charles had purchased from ICRS, International Critical Reactor Systems, after the company had gone into receivership. "When we contacted DARPA," Charles said, "it seemed quite logical that we could plop the SCWO unit onto a guppy and have it in Iraq in 24-hours." He continued, "I was going to bring along a small, self-contained generator set so we wouldn't have to rely on power from the Iraqi grid. Because the reaction is self-sustaining after a propane-fired start-up, we could have completely destroyed every ounce of anthrax that they found, as well as any other biochemical or organic toxin."

"Wouldn't that be overkill?" Cathy asked, showing that she did have knowledge of destruction processes for toxic and hazardous waste.

"Yes, but overkill can be a good thing if the public perceives that this is a sure way to destroy the bugs." He paused. "But, you are right. You probably could kill all of the anthrax in the world simply by using two tons of caustic soda."

Charles and Cathy moseyed down the driveway in between the two metal manufacturing building of HES, Holland Environmental Systems. HES had agreed to store the equipment if they could cannibalize it if DARPA didn't buy the SCWO concept for destruction of anthrax.

And...DARPA didn't buy it. Why? There was no anthrax.

But, with that attempt to work with DARPA, both Weismantels became familiar with the Defense Advanced Research Projects

Administration, and how DARPA had its finger into a host of secret and non-secret, but very quiet, technologies that were moving the government closer and closer into total surveillance of the general public.

Any person's total dossier was digitally available. The Weismantels first discussed this invasion of privacy when, a year earlier, a traffic-monitoring camera was installed at the intersection in front of the Country Store at the corner of Northpark Drive and Free Lane.

At the time, Charles told a group of codgers who drink "old people's" coffee at Howard E. Butt's grocery store each morning, "It's the first step at monitoring your license plate, your face and your whereabouts any time of the day." He was right!

Charles' prediction had been long after that rerun of Colombo.....the one that allowed the trench-coated, cigar-smoking detective to catch a murderer named Derek who had tried to fool a speeding camera located on the Pasadena Freeway North of Los Angeles. The ticket was supposed to create an alibi for the culprit because if he got a speeding ticket on that freeway at the exact same time as the murder was committed, he couldn't have been at the crime scene. But, Colombo caught Derek and his accomplice red-handed.

In fact, DARPA had introduced onto Iraq streets the exact system that worried Charles. DARPA scans and records a person's whereabouts anywhere on the streets of Baghdad. This includes any person that may (or may not) have terrorist ties – or is suspected of having terrorist ties. The system provides facial recognition, including eye imagery scans, and also license plate scans so that U.S. monitors know exactly where a person is traveling, or staying, any time of day or night. All this is quite doable given the heroic speed of the newest Craigs.

Quietly, earlier in the year, in the guise of safety, the U.S. government began to foster a databank called Universal Automotive Identification (UAI) for tracing every licensed vehicle that is on the road. This is similar to cargo location monitoring used by the trucking industry that can trace a package inside a truck anywhere in the world. Yellow Freight, Roadway, and others can tell you exactly where their short or long haul drivers are located anywhere in the lower 48 via satellite tracking. Drivers can be fired if they choose a two-hour stop at a truck stop in Tennessee when that load should have been moving between Chattanooga and Montgomery, or if they stop for a ten-minute nooner at home. The CIA, according to Charles, was moving legislation forward to have the system placed on every vehicle sold in the U.S.

Charles told the HEB coffee clutch that "someday DARPA will be connected to that TV camera at the Country Store and integrating the information with hundreds of other cameras to follow any of you, any time, any place." The ol' guys nodded their heads, but Bob Kater, the king of codgers, ad-libbed: "We'll be dead before then, and if the younger generation doesn't care, it's their problem."

What none of the codgers knew at the time is that the Department of Homeland Security would soon be monitoring every ounce of liquid entering, or trying to enter an airplane. Esoteric as it may seem, there would actually be a TSA Manager of Mild Cologne.

But, considering the Country Store camera, then and there is when Charles decided emphatically that it was time to double his efforts to stop the government's encroachment on privacy. Privately, Cathy shared her husband's thoughts, but publicly they both began to fear that their displays against the president's aggressive policies could lead to problems for the family. But Cathy—wearing her conservative best—encouraged her husband into action by saying many times, "If something is not done today, what will it be like eighty years from now in 2084?"

CHAPTER TWENTY- ONE
2010 – THE OMEGA GROUP

The White family welcomed their new daughter, Alveta, into the world on Saint Patrick's Day, March 17, 2010. Charles and Cathy were the godparents, and the event was made into a double-major event because the same week the White's were also able to move back into their historical home in Galveston on Galveston Island.

The reception was grandiose, and Gerry and Charlie Junior were designated champagne servers. There was food everywhere—and—lots of it—and—that was fortunate—because 99 people consumed 200 bottles of the bubbly. What no one knew is that the bottles were opened near the back fence and each time there was a "pop" it was either CJ or Ger sending a cork-missile into the neighbor's yard. Fortunately the neighbor was there at the party as one of the consumers.

Alveta was the "hit" of the party with her soft golden hair, ultramarine blue eyes, and soul as white as her perfect baptismal gown. She was a little saint, and everyone (except Ger and CJ) wanted to hold her.

The end of the day came and The Weismantels spent the night in the East wing of the home with parents and kids in their own bedrooms and with two water closets serving these guests. The next morning it was a wonderful madhouse with the dads cooking a gigantic breakfast consisting of:

- Grapefruit or melon
- Blueberry pancakes with pure maple syrup
- Zucchini pancakes with sour cream
- Ham steak, bacon and sausage (link and patty)
- Eggs or omelets to order
- Coffee, hot chocolate milk, orange juice
- Homemade biscuits with or without gravy

Mid-morning most of the children went to West beach with older supervising younger—but—Ger and CJ were left to their wits in a completely remodeled garage full of new tools. There they made wooden rubber guns using old tire tubes as the bullets. They sawed out two types....the first used auto tire tubes and had four notches to hold the rubbers using a string to shoot the four bullets. They also made little pistols using a single strip of bicycle tire that acted as the bullet and – the trigger was a spring-loaded clothes pen that would hold the rubber in place. The pistol was fired by releasing the tension on the clothes pen. That way the rubber would pop out and easily shoot across the garage. The guns were wonderful ... but ... as Ger joked: "These would probably be outlawed under HR 45." Both boys laughed, yet both recognized that in the future a person's freedom might depend on gun ownership as granted by the Bill of Rights....haughty thoughts for a couple of teenage Sophomores.

When the serious discussions began inside the house, Ger and CJ found that the bottom step of the staircase would give their ears easy access to every word of parents' conversation without either boy being conspicuous in any way to the adults. These kinds of sessions often led the boys to an understanding of the basis of family beliefs—politically and religiously. Today was the day that parents would spend hours discussing the:

- horrendous spending by the government
- dollar devaluation

- the loss of individual freedoms
- the importance of states' rights

One of the most timely topics in recent weeks, however was City of Houston plans to place 20,000 TV monitors into the homes of families to monitor the activity of children and parents....especially homes that may have special needs or special problems. Both the Whites and the Weismantels had traced this proposed legislation, to, of all things, a 1100 page environmental treatise which had been adopted through Obama legislation that also included carbon dioxide cap-and-trade reasoning and other unconventional concepts.

Charles had long-ago concluded that the green-house-gas legislation was simply a way of passing on taxes to individuals by giving large corporations the ability and authority to pass these costs through to the public by way of monthly utility bills. What most people did not realize however is that also hidden in the fine prints of the document (a document that sat well-placed and well-used on the desk of John

P. Holdren, Obama's Ecoscience guru, was that the government......in the name of environmental controls.......could also adopt selected sterilization programs for specific sections of the population .....or.... the populating as a whole. Thus, the Obama administration had adopted the idea that *Big Brother* could reach out to control the lives of individual citizens (at the government's whim). These same concepts and philosophy had already quietly been adopted in England, and the US move was a step toward globalization.

It was with this background the peers present began to urge Charles to elucidate what he felt was going to happen to the USA ... especially in light of the terrible recession that was all about and the report that the Federal Reserve Bank had actually created as much as $23 Trillion dollars worth of debt in the last three years.....debt that was not tied to the legislative stimulus package (like cash for clunkers)....but simply by giving financial institutions money for free (that was being lent at usury rates). The only voice crying out was a small Texas Congressman by the name of Ron

Paul (who was often debunked by both the GOP and Democrats).

Thus, Charles began his Galveston fireside chat at the home of his best friends – a chat that some might say would be blessed with approval by either a Roosevelt or a Regan.

He began: "Our nation is in a very precarious position. Unfortunately, many of the elected or appointed officials in very powerful positions don't care about the rights of the individual. If a person has a different view, opponents can organize a public relations campaign that can trash you and your family, call you names without substantiation and do almost anything to maim your reputation if you do not agree with the puppeteers. And—who are those that hold the puppet strings? They can be identified by name and by position. I generally refer to them as *The Omega Group*.

"If you study the 'landing place for the trillions of dollars that have been spent by Bush and by Obama, you will find the money in the bank accounts—sometimes hidden accounts—of these *Omega*. If you begin to criticize the Federal Government in respect to the events of the last eighteen months....especially if you begin to do it publicly, there will be a smear campaign to label you as person who believes in conspiracy theories .... and .....governments across the globe would brand you as irrational. But, I have been able to identify real people, and real organizations and real information that ties directly to those benefitting from the economic turmoil. For sure, Alan Greenspan was right in the center of it, and it was he and his cronies like Robert Rubin and Larry Summers who set the stage for a global financial meltdown by allowing certain regulations to be ignored. The changes in laws that allowed the regs to be ignored can be traced to two people—Phil Graham, the senator from Texas, and to his buddy in hiding the influences of deregulation, Bill Clinton."

Charles continued with a frown on his face. "As a registered Republican I find that it is not ironic, it is outright thievery that Henry Paulson left his post as Secretary of Treasury only to take a major position of ownership in a major gold company. What does that tell you about his evaluation of the dollar?" Furthermore, while the Chinese have kept their announcement of choosing a basket of currency for payments of goods and service in the fine print of the newspapers, thier move toward a basket is akin to dollar devaluation. And finally, there is a move to pay for crude oil in currency other than the dollar. That too is going to cause devaluation of the dollar ...and...so far I have not mentioned the many trillions of dollars that have been printed at the St. Louis Federal Reserve Bank that are not part of the legislative spending packages. The latter is simply wholesale printing of money without regard to reserves. Soon, devaluation will inevitably be part of the country's financial picture, and those who are holding dollars will suffer great financial losses. That is one reason why China's sovereign fund is trying desperately to get rid of dollars before they are worth-less"

Charles paused. No one said anything while expecting him to continue.

He did.

"Now that we have had a year to digest the Bush + Obama multi-Trillion dollar bailout, let us take a look at a few of the things that happened ...and...what might be in store.

"First lets look at AIG."

"I like to think of the AIG catastrophe as akin to the story of Jonathan Swift's *Gulliver's Travels* where the people of Laputa needed "flappers" to knock them out of their reverie. In Laputa, the population was entirely absorbed by mathematics, astronomy and music, but they had no practical talents. They were so distracted by theoretical thinking that they needed attendants, called "flappers" to rap them on their mouth or ears to signal when it is their turn to speak or to listen. One might suggest that over the past two decades, US citizens needed a "flap or a flip" on the head to get them to think. Why? Because investors have been letting financial entities rule imperially, pulling down salaries of $104 Million annually at high echelon pay grades and $10 Million manager salaries being commonplace, all this while investors experience omphaloskepsis while spending hours text messaging, or accessing Facebook or Twitter. There is no better example of how this lack of interest in money management led to the debacle at AIG.

"As a chemical engineer, you all know that I look at financial matters much the same way that I look at a chemical plant. If you put a million pounds into the plant....then...a million pounds have to come out....someplace. (Matter cannot be created or destroyed but only changed from one form to another....but....the mass into the plant must equal the mass out). Money acts the same way...If you put a million dollars into the system, it has to come out someplace .... and ...while there is a multiplier effect tied to bank lending, when all the transactions are ended, the books have to balance ... and ... auditors have to assure that money is not being siphoned off into someone's pockets via a Ponzi scheme or downright thievery.

"So, in layman's terms, here is how AIG got into trouble and why the government decided to bail them out. To understand the complications one has to address a financial instrument whose acronym is: CDS, Credit Default Swap. Wikipedia suggests that, in its simplest form, a CDS is a contract, a credit derivative contract, between two counterparties where the "buyer" or "fixed rate payer" makes periodic payments to the "seller" or "floating rate payer." A CDS is a kind of insurance policy tied to debt obligations (often sold in loan stacks of hundreds or thousands and not usually individually) that can experience a profit or loss.

"Banks often work both sides of the CDS market buying CDS protection on the one hand and selling CDS protection at the same time. But, AIG couldn't do that. AIG was only on one side of the transaction....and....this was ok as long as there was no insurance-triggering event....like the housing mortgage meltdown. But...when the crisis hit, AIG was holding more than $440 billion in swaps.....without the necessary reserves

"To exacerbate the problem, just when AIG was being hit by reserve requirements (for all of their CDS), Moody's Investors Service lowered the company's credit rating meaning that AIG had to put up even more collateral to guarantee its ability to pay....but....AIG didn't have any money. So, it turned to the government for help and sold off assets, like its aircraft-leasing business.

"It is fair to ask: How did all of this get going and then snowball?

"According to the *Financial Times*, the genesis of the problem started in 1998 when two members of the J.P. Morgan-Chase credit derivative team – Blyth Masters and Bill Demchak – considered the idea of reducing the amount of reserves (capital needed) to cover possible defaults. By convincing AIG to become involved in the CDS market without carrying the standard rate of reserves, trades set AIG up for insolvency. Quoting the *Financial Times*: "The implications were huge. Banks had typically been forced to hold $800m in reserve for every $10b of corporate loans on their books. Now that sum could fall to just $160m." Called **THE BISTRO CONCEPT**, these financial institutions were able to avoid the normal requirements of international banking rules. Had oversight been initiated by either the US Treasury or the Fed, the gigantic failure could have been avoided, But, Alan Greenspan, who is now former head of the Federal Reserve, kept talking in "Greenspeak," and, with the Grahm-Leach-Bliley laissez-faire Act in place, these two factors acted as seeds of destruction. And.....AIG executives really didn't care, as exhibited by their expenses of $50,000 for spa treatments during their annual business excursion."

Cathy spoke up: "It was 2003 that I remember you saying there was going to be a banking crisis with failures-for-sure and mortgage problems, especially in California where people were buying too much house for their income...including interest-only loans."

"Yes, and all my predications came true. If a simple-minded chemical engineer could see the writing on the wall of Wall Street, you know that the men trading in CDS knew the danger. And, if you really want to chuckle, take a look at this." Charles reached into his briefcase and took out the February 15, 1999 issue of TIME magazine. Everyone in the room began to laugh hysterically as they read the title to the cover story: **THE COMMITTEE TO SAVE THE WORLD**. And -- there on the cover, each with a shit-eating-grin, were Rubin, Greenspan and Summers.

CHAPTER TWENTY- TWO
2020 – NEUTRALIZING THE MONITORS

Charles didn't feel well, but at least he was on the mend.

Standing there, he recognized that for the past three months every part of his body that was within twenty inches of the floor had been hurting at one time or another. This meant from just above the knee down through and including his little toes.....and big toes.

His left knee had swelled and had been so painful that he could barely walk. In a rare move, he visited The Fondren Group to have MD Jean Smith look at the knee cap. An MRI, an x-ray, and an ultrasound proved that the bones were beautiful, which was nice to hear when one is 84 years old, but the starboard (right) sac on his knee was swollen beyond belief because it had been smashed by a stewardess when she was ferociously wheeling her coffee cart down the narrow walking aisle of a 737-B only to clip Charles' slightly exposed knee as the knee angled out into the aisle from seat 22C.

And – just last week — in Saint-Martha-Mary-and-Lazarus Catholic Church parking lot—he had smashed the top of his left foot against a cement tire-stopper. He had reached a level 10 on the pain chart – that's the chart with the little circular, smiling, frowning faces – a Number 10 pain was like someone had smashed the top of the foot with a hammer.......or a knee being hit by an aeroplane food cart careening down the aisle.

And – God forbid – yesterday his right big toe felt like he had the gout – but – how could that be? He had not had any Ben-Franklin-type food for ages. Fortunately today that pain was gone and he was feeling better. "Thank God for Advil," had been his morning prayer.

Good thing he felt better, because CJ was coming over for a "jam" session. Indeed, this was a musical event, but "jam" had become a virtual code word for their organization's secret planning sessions that someday in the future would bring the freedom of the 1950s back to the United States. Charles began to prepare for the visit. He did not want anyone observing the house to see one thing different once CJ and other band members entered the house. Their entry would be two hours from now.

Charles adjusted the drapes on the front windows so that they were open – but not totally open. From the outside, one could see the drapes in the drawn position and slightly— ever so slightly—see through the slats of the Venetian blinds, but without being able to really see what activity was going on inside. The couch that sat in front of the living room window blocked part of the view from the street, so Charles dropped the blinds to a level just below the top of the couch. That way the blinds appeared to be open, but you really could not see inside.

Charles knew that DTC listening devices could still penetrate the room. CJ had learned from the internet that the sensitivity of these acoustical devices could decipher, quite easily, conversations in a normal voice, even when masked by loud music. There would be loud music at this jam, but not a word would be spoken once friendly chit chat and salutations were concluded and the music started.

The music—much of it—would be a tape playing loudly. The participants inside would all be using sign language for the deaf to communicate with one another.

While the drapes were still open, Charles set up the drums, the xylophone, and the speakers and he sat down to play his trumpet trying to emulate Maurey Ferguson's rendition of "*Wild*" – a 78 rpm record he still owned and still played on occasion. Few people still owned phonographs. They were virtual antiques.

From "*Wild*" he moved to a Harry James tune called Delacado. When Betty Grable's husband began the staccato, Charles lips could not handle the accompaniment—especially on high notes. Charles had been able to emulate Harry in years past. He had even belted out *Flight of the Bumble Bee* on the day he and Cathy were married in 1980.

Gosh, how he missed her. Her death two years ago had left him devastated and with no reason at all to fear for his life. That is when he approached his son Charlie Junior with his plan. He had cautioned CJ from the very beginning, but Charlie Junior wanted to be part of it. How ironic that most of their detailed discussions took place while father and son were enjoying their favorite pastime—fishing—at The Point.

Charles had placed a fishing pole into CJ's hands even before CJ could walk. Charles and Cathy would go down to the Kingwood duck pond near the little league fields and put Charlie Junior's old playpen near the edge of the water. It had a masonite bottom. CJ could pull himself up to the side of the pen, and he would do that heroic standup—at least it was heroic for a baby—on the side of the playpen facing the water. Charles would stick a very long, light bamboo pole into the pen so that it actually hung out over the water. There was a ten foot fishing line tied to the end of the pole – with no hook. Even at one year old, CJ actually thought he was fishing.

When Charles caught a blue gill, or as Boudreaux, the Coon-Ass from Lafayette called them – a bream – he would toss the fish onto the masonite floor of the playpen, and the fish would flip and flop and baby CJ would reach down with one hand and try to pick up the fish while holding on to the side of the playpen with his other hand. This act was precarious for a toddler who still did not have eye-leg-foot-hand coordination, and the fish kept getting away until CJ stomped (his right leg was always his stompin' leg.....and...his right shoe was always his stompin' shoe. I mention this because it—the right shoe—always required a good cleaning after a fishing trip) on the fish and stunned him so badly that the finned prize became pick-up-able by an infant.

Those kind of fun days spiced the family activity through the end of the century, but the dramatic changes that took place after 9-11 – the dramatic loss of freedom that evolved from the elections of 2004 – the dramatic, terrible controls that the federal government initiated in the name of protecting people from terrorism – these changes made the incarceration of Japanese-Americans during World War II look like a kindergarten play. Charles' friend, Martha Akeama, had related these stories of her family's ordeal behind the cyclone fences, isolated in the high desert. They were horrendous. But so were today's stories of Michelene Abboud, a Lebanese Christian, who the DTC was monitoring 24-hours a day because of her long-time technical association with Shaharon Shavell, a Muslim chemical engineer, living in Kuwait. Shaharon, a scientist, could easily formulate bombs for terrorists.   Shaharon was now living and teaching in Kuwait, but his trips to the United States were often, and he always met with Abboud.   The DTC was on her like syrup covering a pancake.

Both Charles and Cathy had met Shaharon in New Orleans in April, 2004, at the World Filtration Congress sponsored by the National Filter Society. Abboud had arranged a dinner meeting and brought Shaharon to the dinner. That night they all had observed and recognized and knew that an *Omega*-monitor had recorded the meeting, and from that time forward Charles, Cathy and now, Charlie Junior, were closely watched by the Department of Homeland Security and eventually by the DTC.

Surveillance teams in Sprint trucks were often identified near the Weismantels' Kingwood homes. Charles got wind of the surveillance when his neighbor, who worked for Sprint, came across the camouflaged DTC van in his own neighborhood where he was supposed to be working. The neighbor checked out the van and immediately determined that it was not Sprint at all, but the DTC.

Following that episode, all Weismantels assumed, rightfully, that they had tails wherever they went.

CHAPTER TWENTY- THREE
2047 – LAISSE FAIRE

Charlie Junior looked out his front window and saw the SBC truck drive by. He knew that these trucks were often a front for GEORGE, so this drive-by worried him. He also disliked SBC for other reasons.

SBC had merged with Sprint in a "friendly" takeover, and in the process over forty thousand Sprint employees had lost their jobs. The telephone industry was now ruled by only two large communication giants, both in bed with the White House, and the efforts years ago to break up AT&T and create widespread competition had, in fact, led to a 500% increase on the average phone bill of each household in the U.S. With state PUC's playing the role of a politician's fundraising committee, telephone bills, electricity prices and natural gas costs skyrocketed as did the political donations and off-budget support aid to the coffers of incumbents.

Ever since Alveta died last year, Charlie Junior often found himself staring out the front window, daydreaming. Losing the one you love—love with all your heart—creates a void—

a void that has no entrance or exit—a void that, on earth, can remain empty siglos de los siglos. Charlie Junior felt that void whenever he reminisced. It was an emptiness like being hungry but never being able to eat. It hurt. It hurt the stomach. It hurt the heart. The mind hurt and the soul hurt – especially the soul because the graces that come from everyday love, the graces from conjugal love, and the graces of a simple touch are not available. Alveta was only 36 when she died from unknown complications stemming from severe stomach spasms.

He continued to stare out the window when the phone rang. He answered, using the three words he often used when answering the phone: "Charlie Junior speaking." [And—he often said: *Bueno*].

The line was dead.

He looked at his caller ID, but there was no identification. His brow, previously ruffled due to thoughts of Alveta was now ruffled due to worries that GEORGE was checking on his whereabouts. He knew he was being watched just like his dad had been watched by governmental officials years earlier. All chemical engineers were watched. All chemical engineers were monitored. All chemical engineers were suspected terrorists because they were easily the most knowledgeable to build WMD's.

CJ remembered that night, years ago, when, as a child, he heard his mother utter words that a holocaust would come to the U.S. Her prediction had been subtly true as police frequently beat Muslims, or people that looked like Muslims, with night sticks. Blacks were often the brunt of these beatings if they had Islamic names, and what irony existed in California. There, near Bishop, were Islamic camps where U.S. citizens – no one knew how many – were being held hostage, without bail, without contact with the outside world – in an area very close to where Japanese-Americans had been held captive during WWII. The ACLU, LULAC, and worldwide human rights groups were all attempting to find out who had been apprehended and why. The reason given to anyone by government sources was simply: "Suspected terrorism." Habeas Corpus had virtually been taken out of U.S. dictionaries.

The U.S. military had tripled in size since the second Bush, although Bush II was the one that had set those growth-in-military-personnel into motion. It was not the National Guard that increased in size, but rather, the RA and hiring of mercenaries. Increased public rancor and confrontations became rampant. There were real concerns that anyone might be thrown into jail for real or contrived reasons, and such concerns were not make-believe. So called "conservatives" had introduced legislation and Constitutional Amendments to outlaw The National Rifle Association and the possession of guns by the public even though the Supreme Court ruling of 2008 said that Washington, DC ordnances outlawing handguns was unconstitutional. The proposed legislation did not mention NRA per se, but, effectively there was a Congressional move, backed by the president, to delete the second amendment to the Constitution on the basis that anyone owning a gun was a potential terrorist. What years ago might have been the platform of a liberal Democrat became the obsession of Republicans.

Why?

The military did not want the public to have weapons of any kind for obvious reasons. They were preparing for combat with citizens.

Charlie Junior was right in the middle of GEORGE's watchdog maneuvers because he had inherited chemical engineering expertise from both his mom and dad, and as president of White Cloak Paint, Varnish & Lacquer LLC, he and his company had major access to almost any toxic or hazardous chemical; any petroleum solvent, ketone or acetate; or any grade of nitrocellulose as well as carbon, sulfur and saltpeter, the basic ingredients for gunpowder. Yes, an unmarked van in front of his home was cause for alarm.

It was no secret that both he and his neighbors shared a common worry that both the U.S. and state governments had become entirely too powerful, quietly usurping everyday rights in the name of national security. Worst of all, at the federal level, Congress had abrogated its right to declare war, surrendering that decision to the president who time and time again made decisions that were totally belligerent. Congress had given a rubber stamp to the president to investigate anyone, even without a warrant. The rights of the individual were being totally ignored, and strange bedfellows, such as the ACLU and true conservatives, began to sleep together.

CHAPTER TWENTY- FOUR
2004 – SHIITE HUMILIATION

Rice had testified before the committee investigating 9-11.

The press had done their analysis of her testimony.

Analysts had carefully used the word "Doctor" when referring to Rice, and,

Saturday Night Live (SNL) had a heyday with Janet Jackson playing the part of "Condee" complete with a half inch space between her two front teeth, and comical instructions to "bare all" if the investigators' questions of the SNL Congressional Committee got too hard to handle.

The only problem was: The Saturday Night Live show was not really funny to Charles and Cathy. The skit was too close to the truth. Cathy turned off the TV, stared at Charles and said, "What are we going to do?" She didn't mean the USA. She meant herself and her husband.

She asked the question because the two of them had politics and Iraq on their mind right now and Iraq was a conversation topic almost every hour they were together. Last week, the killing and mutilation of four civilians working in Iraq was fresh in their minds. Indeed, this terror and other horrific events, so violently covered by news media made the Weismantels wonder if many more staged killings would be the goal of both Sunis and Shiites alike.

"What are we going to do?" Charles repeated her question in preparing to answer it. "We are going to do what we always do...vote conservative and vote our conscience."

Charles continued. "I spoke to John Browning this week for almost an hour. It was the first time I had spoken to him in almost ten years. His call, unexpected, was a delight."

Charles stood up and walked across the Western-style living room. The long side of the room ran east to west.....or west to east....or....all west if you were from Texas. The room used its furniture to separate it into two separates sections with each section housing two sets of couches and two sets of large chairs, two sets of ottomans, two knee-high coffee tables and two areas for two sets of people to carry on two sets of conversations. Tonight it was only Charles and Cathy in the West wing.

"John has been a conservative Republican as long as I've known him, but he is really worried about Bush, and he is even more worried about Dick Cheney. He thinks Cheney is a thief and works only for a choice few amongst *The Omega Group*." He paused, "Ironically, when I was getting the tags for the Marquis, I stopped at a table in front of the court house where a man was handing out literature from backers of Lyndon LaRouche. That literature suggests that Cheney is the real president guiding Pentagon warlords and that Bush is Cheney's pawn."

"Isn't LaRouche the fellow who ran for president eight times?" Cathy asked.

"Yes," Charles replied, "and, while he's definitely weird, he seems to understand who makes up *The Omega Group*. He has done a thorough analysis of sovereign wealth funds and the connection between them and *Omega*."

Cathy looked concerned. She was about to speak, but before doing so, many of their previous husband-wife conversations flashed through her mind. She and Charles thrashed things out thoroughly before making decisions that would affect them and the seven children.

Sure, only four were still living at home, but everyone stayed in close contact and each person's opinion carried value.

It is amazing how many thoughts can flash through one's mind in a split second of time. Cathy's brain had processed three previous tête-à-têtes with her husband. In those tetes, Cathy and Charles had already concluded that very few senators or congressmen had a backbone. This was because the Weismantels believed that only Congress has the right to declare war. By passing a law that gave invasion prerogatives to the president, each member of the house and each senator had abandoned their responsibility as an elected official. Charles had said: "If there had had to be a Congressional head count, we never would have gone to war." Cathy agreed, suggesting such abrogation was unconstitutional.

Both Cathy and Charles were strong fiscal conservatives, and it was obvious that Bush was the biggest spender since Ronald Reagan, whose spending policies the Weismantels abhorred. During one of their past conversations, they agreed that a Democrat,

Bill Clinton, had been the most fiscally responsible president in recent years......and that was because he constantly had Billy Archer, House Chairman of Ways and Means, looking over his shoulder.

Under the Republicans, government employment was growing faster than under any recent president, Republican or Democrat.

In the name of protecting people against terror, the federal government now had the ability to monitor every digital action that you initiated every minute of the day while coupling this to online monitoring of you or your auto anytime, any place. Both of them had often used the expression: "Big Brother is watching you now!" This reference was to Orwell's 1984. These thoughts flashed through her mind, and then Cathy spoke.

"Sweetheart, I think we are near anarchy, and I fear a takeover by the military."

There was silence.

Then she continued.

"Spurred by hawks, the cowboys in Washington are likely to invade anyone on whatever grounds they decide. There is a good chance we will go into Iran as Congress sits idly, exacerbating a situation created by administrative dictatorship and by a legal system that answers to the highest bidder." She stopped, and then added, "Israel will do the dirty work."

Charles looked at her and answered with one word.

"Profound," he said.

And then he asked, "So, what is the answer?"

"I don't know. I don't know." She answered twice for emphasis.   She answered twice because she was befuddled.   She answered twice and then said, "But this I do know.   The stupidity of an Iranian war is tied to a complete naivety of the administration about the Middle East, virtual darkness by congress in respect to Islam, and a total breakdown of intelligence and understanding of the history of the area by both the CIA and the FBI."

This mouthful of words spit forth in less than fourteen seconds and was followed by: "Even an idiot should have been able to count the number of Shiites in Iraq and know that their loyalty is always tied to their religious leaders and," she paused, "Iraqi leaders are Siamesed to Iran."

She paused and continued her soliloquy. "Even an idiot knows how Shiites think and have seen their fanaticism on religious holidays by slicing their foreheads with razors to bleed in unity with their deceased, martyred brethren and others of their sect." Without a pause she hastened to add, "Even an idiot should have understood the humiliation Shiites would feel when foreigners, when infidels ruled the streets of their Islamic state. Saddam had kept this under control by fear, oppression, police action and military might. Are we so short sighted that we forgot that we were the ones giving him bullets ... bullets meant to keep Iran under control?"

"Besides," she continued, "when will people realize that Islam is not just a religion, but is also a totalitarian political system built on tyranny."

Charles did not say a word.

Cathy spit out more sentences. "Didn't anyone have enough sense to do the numbers and understand that almost seventy percent of the Persians are loyal to Iranian religious ideology?

"The people advising the President of the United States are idiots!"

She paused for a long time. Tears filled her eyes and she ended her tirade: "We have just begun to see the holocaust that will be part of our lives for years to come. I am afraid that much of it will be on our own soil and will be our own fault."

Charles took her into his arms. They held one another. Not another word was spoken.

As they turned to go upstairs, there, quietly, standing for how long they did not know, was little Charlie Junior. The eight year old may have heard every word they had uttered.

The three of them melted together, went up the stairs, and climbed into the king-sized bed, CJ in the middle.

CHAPTER TWENTY- FIVE
2030 – THE FED

CJ had hunkered down in the big easy chair that had been in the White's living room as long as he had been alive—at least it seemed so. With the Galveston sunlight reflecting off the Gulf of Mexico waters, it was 10:00 AM, and the solar rays poured through the picture window providing all the lumens that CJ needed to read the front page of the Galveston County Daily News. While still at the front page, he spoke loudly to Gerry who was out of sight in the kitchen making coffee. Gerry was the only one in the family who had not gone to California for Alveta's graduation.

"It is hard to believe." Charlie Junior paused in his high decibel communication to Gerry. Then, he repeated himself. "It is hard to believe that it has been twenty-three years since the sub-prime mortgage debacle and we still have not resolved key issues that caused the problems."

Gerry stuck his head around the door jam and quizzed, "What'd you say?"

CJ pounded his index finger three times upon the open newspaper pointing directly at the article he was reading—the lead story on the front page, and, then he answered Gerry saying, "We are still arguing about what caused the sub-prime mortgage debacle!" Then, he straightened out the paper that had been bent from all his pointing and prodding so that he could continue reading the who, what, when, where, why and how.

"It says 'The U.S. has still not recovered from the inadequacies of the financial institutions that were responsible for the sub-prime mortgage fiasco of 2007....and......U.S. and European banks....at least the stockholders...still feel the pinch of the poor management decisions that made millions for the managers while stockholders lost billions.'" CJ remembered his dad saying "We all trusted the smart guys.....but Greenspan was asleep at the switch." His dad was referring to Alan Greenspan who headed THE FED when all of the bad loans were made.

The managers of the financial institutions, and the U.S. Treasury and the U.S. Federal Reserve System never once raised a red flag to stop the nonsense of selling bad loans time and time again with no one applying principles of risk management.

CJ paused and with a disgruntled grunt said in a pathetic way: "THE FED!"

With this, Gerry shrugged his shoulders and returned to the kitchen. CJ closed his eyes and snuggled the back of his head into the corner of the chair where the chair-back met its side. He began to think out loud. "It does not take a genius to understand that a person should not overextend themselves when buying a home. Greenspan understood what was going on. He understood the funds flow from one financial institution, to another, to another, with each step of the money movement becoming more camouflaged from the public. The implications - misunderstood or misrepresented by THE FED - still implies tacit approval of what was going on." There! He had satisfied himself, but not entirely. This is because he believed that *The Omega Group* somehow had their finger in the sub-prime pie, and he believed that 'if you always follow the dollars and who is getting them' you will come to conclusions that you never see without doing a financial overview.

Gerry walked into the room holding two cups of black coffee and handed CJ one of them and then added a verbal analysis of his own. "I have always felt that Bush-Two was beholden to special interest groups and that he, as president, had no earthly idea of how THE FED interfaced with The Treasury nor did he understand the double entry bookkeeping tie-ins between THE FED and the Treasury."

CJ looked at him with a question mark all over his face. CJ asked himself: Was this Gerry talking? Even after years of friendship, CJ did not know that those kinds of thoughts were rolling through Gerry's brain. But before CJ could answer his own question, Gerry continued to mumble, "If I let my mind meander, there are other things that bother me about the last two of the George W. years", and with that Gerry began to tic off a list of things that were obviously NOT spur-of-the moment musings. They included a history of 2007 and 2008:

- The U.S. Balance of Payments problems exacerbated by trade complications.......especially with China
- How coffers of oil-rich countries became very full of dollars when paying for oil

turned to a basket of currencies (the U.S. dollar, the Euro and the Yuan) rather than using the U.S. dollar for crude payments. This move-to-the-basket increased oil prices by 30% in the U.S

- Russian energy interests exacerbating U.S. oil prices
- The importance of "sovereign investments" leading to foreign ownership of U.S. banks, real estate and oil fields in the lower 48

Gerry explained his thinking that all of the above created a domino effect in respect to dollar devaluation. In respect to devaluation, the national debt skyrocketed leading to an unannounced, but, de-facto, devaluation of the dollar hastened by the trillion-dollar-plus trade deficit.

Gerry had been listing all of these economic facets as facts and then he stopped and looked at Charlie Junior as if he were an attorney facing a judge asking for the death penalty, and he said, "As a result of all this, we are now paying $200 per barrel for crude oil, the price of corn and soy beans has doubled in the last eighteen months........again......and there is an additional squeeze on the real income and disposable income of the middle class. Overall, this results in a lower income for most U.S. citizens. Only the top income levels have benefited."

"You mean, *The Omega Group*?" Charlie Junior was goading Gerry to say yes. CJ had mentioned this group many times to Gerry to include how *Omega* was an extension of Yale's secret Order of the Skull and Bones, a group with tremendous financial influence and whose members manipulated money as if they were playing Monopoly. These men historically included those tied to international banking such as W.A. Harriman, Knight Wooley and Prescott Bush, the father of George H.W. Bush. There were also ties to both of the Rothschild Banks in the UK and Germany, Lazard Brothers in France and IMS in Italy.

Gerry looked at Charlie Junior and said, "I forget which Supreme Court Justice said it, and the quote may not be perfect, but, it goes something like this: 'The real rulers in Washington are invisible and exercise all of their power behind the scenes.' It is these invisible puppeteers that hold the power over our lives. So, yes - I agree with you. *The Omega Group* is alive and well and controls much more than any of us ever suspected."

Charlie Junior asked Gerry, "Can the problems be identified and solved by better education?"

Gerry hesitated to answer, but, quietly began to provide a thinking-out-loud reply. "Last year, when the Rohm & Haas Division of Dow closed all of its Houston Ship Channel operations where the wages ranged from $30 to $50 per hour, three thousand employees lost their jobs. These people were typically 28 to 58 years old. I don't think that they found relief in soothsayers suggesting that the answer to their unemployment problem is 'become better educated', especially when Republicans are still trying to eliminate Pell Grants and student loans."

Gerry knew that Charlie Junior was a registered Republican.

"The reality of these job losses is tied to the reality of globalization, an era where highly paid people are destined for lower incomes and where many highly educated will join the ranks of the unemployed or underutilized. I'm thinking about the degreed IBM middle-classsers that faced walking-the-plank at IBM when Big Blue sent their jobs—thousands of them—to India. And, consider how the U.S. glass industry has downsized. When Anchor Hocking closed its factories, who wanted to hire the man or woman that was working as an operator or QC-checker on the annealing lehr? What can they be trained or retrained to do? And the sad part is that plates and stoneware being imported probably have lead pigments as part of the formulation......and we are eating off those plates!

"It makes me ask two questions: Who owns the world?...and...Who Controls the World?" Gerry stopped talking.

Charlie Junior knew the answers to both of Gerry's questions, but he could not say anything. He could not tell Gerry that the problem the U.S. was facing was much more than financial puppeteering. There were bad guys at the top that were willing to resort to military action—willing to kill people—to get what they wanted.

CHAPTER TWENTY-SIX
2079 – THE GATHERING STORM

"Saupo!"

Charlie Junior heard the word shouted from Chuck's disgruntled baritone belly.

Chuck had yelled it, almost at the top of his deep voice, and, even before Charlie Junior could react, Chuck screamed it out again ...... "Saupo!!"

In a much calmer manner than his son's, CJ asked: "What in the world is Sappo?"

"It's not Sappo, Dad.....It's Saupo."

"Well then, let me rephrase my question. What the devil is Saupo?"

Chuck looked at him. His Dad was waiting for a reply. Three seconds passed, then three more, when finally, CJ looked at his son with a question mark all over his face. It was then Chuck responded.

"It means everything!......It means nothing!......It is the kind of word that is an expletive suitable for any occasion. It is the perfect word for what happened today."

As he finished his sentence, Chuck held up a light yellow copy of the *Financial Times*.

Years earlier, the paper had been printed on pink newsprint—almost a parchment—but the editors received so many complaints from their U.S. readers about the pink background being hard to read that the stateside version of the *Financial Times* switched to a yellow base colored newsprint and the change was received with thunderous applause. The change was particularly important to those wearing trifocals.

After the color change, both subscriptions and subscription renewal blossomed, even to a younger sect. That is when CJ introduced Chuck to *Financial Times*. He told his son, "*Financial Times* editors have an entirely different perspective on what is going on in the world compared to *The Washington Post*, *The Washington Times*, and *The New York Times*." Chuck's dad said that the latter three always seemed to eat the pabulum served to them by flaks—both governmental PR deceivers and corporate public relations departments alike.

Recently, the flak-guns were firing-for-effect at the U.S. Senate, where this smaller-but-more-powerful body of the bilateral was involved in a heated debate on the constitutionality of giving the president the right to declare war without a one-by-one tally of members of Congress. The idea was to avoid another Iraq when Congress virtually abrogated their job to declare war. The legislation was pointed; it would not give a war-declaration-right so that the president could act unilaterally.

The debate had been long-lasting, but not filibustered. Ever since George W. Bush had sent troops into Iraq based on faulty G-2 (coupled to hawkish ideals that had little regard for the life or death of Muslims), a small group of conservative Southern Democrats and a smaller group of Goldwater-type Republicans yearly tried to pass legislation that would assure Congress actually did the war-voting according to their constitutional mandate and assure that congress did not hand that privilege over to "an emperor."

Taft, one of the GOP-group, stumped his state, and the nation saying:

"Never again Tripoli!

"Never again Viet Nam!

"Never again Somalia!

"Never again Afghanistan!

"Never again Iraq!

"Never again The Philippines!"

The Philippines was just the latest troop deployment by the United States in what the locals referred to as the Ugly Americans, where unlike the cheers and palm branches the Filipinos gave to General Douglas McArthur, this time the entire population of the country was disgruntled by the continual presence of thousands of American soldiers occupying the Island of Jolo with no military success in sight. Ever since 1993, Jolo had been a Muslim militant stronghold and the island remained so even after seven decades of Americans trying to find and beat the gorillas.

The Abu Sayyaf Group, or Father of the Sword, also known as Al-Harakat or Al-Islamiyya, had broadened its Jemaah Islamiyah (Islamic Community) base at the expense of Christianity. Christians also became passive— even helpful—to the Muslim Mindanao's of the country if only to avoid being beheaded. The U.S. was in the middle of another Iraq.

However, even with the "Never, Never, Never" slogans ringing under the Capital's Dome, national legislative action pointed toward another Congressional abrogation, again gifting war OKs to the White House. This fact made the front page of the *Financial Times*, and Chuck's reaction was emphatic:

"Saupo!!"

CHAPTER TWENT-SEVEN
2080 – THE HINGE OF FATE

Election year, 2080, did not start out with a bang. Instead, the six Democratic candidates and the four Republican candidates squared off in early-to-mid-2079, pointing their rifles at the Arizona primary that now took place always two weeks before the Iowa caucus. Earlier, and earlier, and earlier, the run for the White House became a drudgenary yoke on the public, with millions of dollars being spent by the latest twist in political action committees, or PACs. The new money-method was known as MACs, or Monetary Action Committees, a private funding service with virtually no controls or oversights. The MAC could be both a politician's and a lobbyist's best friend. It was a method for politicians, and particularly supporters of incumbents, to spend millions of dollars without accountability. Bludgeonary attacks reached TV. Many ads were blatant attacks, with false messages, aimed at first-time candidates.

As the 51 states, DC, and territories-protectorate prepared to elect convention delegates, the divisions within the registered voters was not so much along the lines of parties, but rather, along a religious focus, namely those who accept Muslims as true Americans and those who don't. The shadow of 9-11 was alive and well, and the 9-11 message was tied to fear and to what must be done to assure the nation was without terror and without terrorists. Some politicians actually promoted annihilation, or at least some form of alienation of Muslims, perhaps taking away voting privileges for certain sects. One senator wailed: "Where is Jesse Helms when you need him?"

There was to be an expansion of the World War II type Japanese-American incarceration for entire Muslim sects. Some suspects were, without warrant, actually placed near Bishop, California near the same site where the Japanese had lost all rights in the 1940s.

The deportation option was widely discussed. This topic raised its serpent head on both Congressional floors. Some versions would go so far as to affect Lebanese and Orthodox Christians. Never before had politics and religion been so intertwined and tied to fear and distrust. Individual freedoms were at stake, and under the majority rules, one could see that the majority might act uncontrollably. This included the president.

The Bill of Rights was constantly under attack, not so much by individuals, but by politicians who claimed to represent individuals who would (wanted to) deny rights to certain minorities. This attack was done openly or sometime through cloak-and-dagger methods.

Many people did not seem to mind the attacks on religious freedom–as long as it was not their religion that was being attacked. But, defacto, all religious freedom promised under the U.S. Constitution was under attack.

Feeling safe with the Judeo reasoning at Jericho or the Christianity of the Spanish Inquisition became problematic. In reality, religious apartheid had become ramped in the U.S., especially if you were Muslim. Even more so if you were a Black Muslim.

Entering into this 2080, Chuck found himself afraid....afraid that democracy was about to fail.

Why? Because the majority that rules, regardless of whether the majority is a donkey or an elephant, would reflect the will of the majority—a majority that might easily justify the imprisonment, torture or even the killing of

American citizens that believe in a Deity that is not Judeo-Christian.

Chuck, a Republican, was ready to vote for a Democrat in this general election on this second Tuesday In November because all the GOP candidates were sure to try to concentrate unlimited power within the presidency. Chuck, as well as his father, felt that electing any of the Republicans would move the country further away from the rights of the individual.

Barry Goldwater was rolling over and over and over in his grave. Ironically, it was the Republicans who were considering legislation limiting a citizen's right to bear arms. A Weismantel adage for many years was: "Beware of the President who takes away your guns." Chuck knew that the post script to taking away guns is that the government is trying to control you.

The year moved through October and through November. The election results led to Republicans getting prepared for the inauguration.

CHAPTER TWENT- EIGHT
2081 – TRIUMPH OR TRAGEDY

Somewhere…

Somewhere known only to a few………….

The Omega Group celebrated the GOP win………..

They celebrated <u>exactly</u> the same as if a Democrat would have won the election.

The triumphant would be leading the country into a belligerent condition pitting religion against religion, neighbor against neighbor, brother against brother, and friend against friend.

The world's insurance system was falling apart on the basis of threats and fears as well as actual terrorist attacks and bombings, mostly in the near East and in the Middle East. Always there were fears of anyone against another. The "bad guys" became so sophisticated that NORAD feared being shut down or controlled by a smart hacker with a portable Dell.

The situation was so alarming that Sam Woodbury suggested that CJ should send Chuck to Washington to monitor what was happening. Chuck made the trip and using a flux monitor and electronic router set up in the bell tower of St. Joseph's Church at 313 2nd Street NE in DC, began to intercept encrypted messages between the Pentagon, Congressional offices and the White House. Charlie Junior had suggested that church because of its proximity to key governmental communication paths. CJ suggested that it was not important to specifically decipher and translate messages. Rather, the first importance was to know the sender and the recipient. Identifying these parities would give Chuck an understanding of which people were planning clandestine acts even without having the infrastructure or having the decoding information of messages flowing through the electronic routes.

What Chuck learned is that there were four key players within the Pentagon—all presidential appointees—that were communicating heavily with three key generals of the Army and the Marine Corps, in concert with the Secretary of Defense, The Attorney General, The Secretary of State, and the President himself.

The Navy did not seem to be involved with the planned operations to attack U.S. citizens.

Chuck assumed that the approaching Armageddon would not involve ships. In a one-if-by-land, and, two-if-by-sea, structure, what we were likely to be experiencing was a "1."

What Chuck didn't know was where military action would take place or when. His guess was that any major increase in electronic messages would tell him which unit would be called on to act–which units would be activated by the president.

But what would the soldiers be asked to do? Therein may lay the tragedy.

CHAPTER TWENT- NINE
2082 – CLOSING THE RING

After Chuck returned from DC, he met Charlie Junior in the White Cloak parking lot and, walking to the Mustang that was parked under a large live oak, they sat inside and passed notes to one another. This was SOP in case voice monitors were trained on them or if there was a bug nearby.

Chuck handed CJ the first note written on the front of a HIGHLAND 3M sticky pad. They would pass the little square yellow sheet back and forth keeping it out of view from anyone that might be observing them sitting there in the automobile.

"Dad: I think we need to have a group meeting at the Park Ranger circle. Everything points toward a move by the President to a call to bear arms. My first guess is they would call up a unit from Kansas, but my second guess is that the unit may be Marines. I don't think anyone in Congress suspects what he is about to do."

"Son, that's a pretty serious activation. Are you sure that now is the time he will make such a drastic move?"

"The frequency of transmission has reached an all-time high—especially to the Secretary of Defense who is the most likely person to recommend pulling the trigger. And he's a hothead in the mold of Donald Rumsfeld."

"Pulling the trigger on whom?"

"We are not sure, but everything points toward one of the U.S. cities that has a large population of Muslims."

"Soon?"

"If you mean, will it be tomorrow, I can't answer that for sure, but I believe it is time for our dry run because we certainly are not more than eighteen months away. It will most likely be soon after Congress passes the Antiterrorist Act. That passage will give the president the right to attack anyone, anywhere......and.......to kill anyone who is a minority."

"I'll call the meeting."

Charlie Junior completed the last note, picked it up along with all the others and placed all the notes in an old metal cowbell...a real one that had been used on real cows to monitor bovine location. The bell had been sitting on the floor of the old Mustang along with a welder's glove.

Putting the notes into the bell, Charlie Junior opened the windows of the 'stang and started the notes on fire using the cigarette lighter, holding the bell with the welder's glove

Chuck had reached the door of the plant, turned to look at his dad, and he nodded. They both knew that it would not be long before years of protection-planning would become reality.

CHAPTER THIRTY
2083 – THE SADDEST HOUR

Congress was hotly debating legislation known as the "Antiterrorist Act of 2083." When the bill appeared in the Federal Register, it created a furor amongst average citizens, but the average citizen had lost control over senators and house members. In control were lobbyists who took showers in money from earmark legislation that exacerbated financial deficits. Red ink was inevitable. Inflation was real.

The Antiterrorist bill assuredly had the necessary votes to become law. The current president, a clone of the late George W. Bush, wanted this legislation badly so that he could unilaterally control all military action against terrorists, suspected terrorists—either home or abroad—and without any oversight.

Traditional bastions of human rights had good reason for concern. Just like with the Iraq war, where both houses of Congress gave the president the right to declare war, this new legislation expanded presidential powers giving the man in the oval office carte blanche approval to carry on attacks within the fifty-one states. The Antiterrorist Act of 2083 gave the current president—or any future president—the right to use the military to attack, under the guise of war, individuals, organizations, terrorists or suspected terrorists on U.S. soil without seeking the approval of Congress.

True conservatives were blistering mad at the proposal and pointed to numerous occasions where federal "good guys" were, in fact, pawns of *The Omega Group*, although they didn't mention *The Omega Group* by name. Federal "bad guys" without a true devotion to constitutional and individual rights seemed to have the votes to pass the Act. The powerbrokers had married the legislation to financial gain beyond belief. The bill had over 100 earmarks. The Act would make spending in Iraq look like chickenfeed. And on the home front, big business would be making billions and billions of profit-dollars.

The bill passed easily.

CHAPTER THIRTY-ONE
2084 – FEBRUARY 14, AM

It had been a long time coming, but the fears and the displays of antagonism against Muslims, the reappearance of skinheads, and the ever-pounding drumbeating by the press—a press closely monitored and vicariously intertwined with the federal government—had led to fires in Detroit...real fires...and firebombs maliciously thrown, and obviously contrived, by enemies of Islam. The seeds of hatred and mistrust had been planted carefully so that any forceful intervention that might occur would be accepted, nationwide, as a logical and a worthy attempt to combat terrorism.

It began on Thursday, February 14, 9:00 AM, at the Islamic Mosque on Grosse Pointe Avenue in Detroit. Anyone should have seen it coming, especially the victims, but no one—not local police—not local TV—and no newspaper editor questioned the move of a company of Marines and their tanks from Camp Pendleton, California into Detroit, Michigan—supposedly for winter training experience and to experience winter training conditions.

No one said: "Why train in Detroit? Why not Alaska?" But, there were 14 tanks, railroaded across the Sierras, across the Rockies and into Detroit, totally without fanfare.

When these diesel-fueled war machines moved into the city streets, it was a total surprise to everyone to listen to the roar of engines and the treads of the M50 that cut into the cement and asphalt streets. The metal, mobile cannons supported a cavalry of war. Armored personnel carriers moved from the spokes of central city outward on 15th Street and into the heavily populated Muslim neighborhoods. The mission had the express intent of destroying the city's six main Mosques.

In an unbelievable show of force against its own U.S. citizens, both those born here or naturalized, the commander and troops arrived at their destination across from the Mosque, and a Captain took the bullhorn and bellowed: "Attention in the Mosque of Mohammad Mohammad: Please exit the building with your hands raised in the position of surrender and you will not be harmed. We caution you, do not resist arrest or your life will be endangered." The bellowing continued for 15 minutes and then the tone of the commander changed as did his message.

People on the sidewalks stood aghast at what was happening before their eyes. This couldn't be happening in the United States, but it was. Some of those lining the sidewalks noticed that about half of the soldiers were dressed like Marines but were, in fact, wearing the shoulder patch of Blackwater-Xe. These were mercenaries hired by the federal government, who were about to kill U.S. citizens. This was a far cry from border-patrol duties, but, Blackwater-Xe forces took orders directly from the oval office.

Eight decades of homeland security, was about to erupt in destruction of U.S. citizens on our home soil by our own military and a band of mercenaries. [Nikita Khrushchev, wherever he may be, is pounding his shoe and laughing hysterically].

A few people came out of the Mosque and were immediately incarcerated, taken into semi-tractor trailer trucks with no air supply that carried the logo: "Rent it from Hertz." As civilians were horded into the trucks, one could see the fear and the astonishment on their faces.

Then, in an amazing attack, the tank commander demanded that everyone leave the building before it was blown up. In just ten minutes, the bombardment started without a Marine or a Blackwater-Xe-paid employee entering the building. After the mosque took 20 rounds of 60-millimeter cannon shells from each tank, virtually no stone was left standing upon a stone. Anyone inside was either dead or covered in rubble lying inside a suffocating bath of bricks. Not even a wailing wall was left intact.

The Hertz semi-tractor trailer doors were shut, encasing the Muslims like migrant workers crossing the Rio Grande. The vehicle drove off. To where, no one could tell.......no one knew.

The Marines left. The Blackwater-Xes left. There was no examination of the rubble. It had become a massive grave. If the gigantic pile contained life, that life was buried deeply among the fragments of masonry and toppled spirals. Listening carefully, there were no moans of death. It was our own 9-11.

As quickly as they arrived, the Marines and the Blackwater-Xes headed to their next Detroit destination to repeat the maneuver–a horror that might only be imagined, but unbelievably was taking place in real life, right here in the USA.

The nation was at war – with itself.

Chuck sat, stunned, glaring at the roll top desk while asking himself: Where did our country go wrong? What was the tipping point of no return? Searching his memory bank, he reached forward into one of the cubby holes of the desk and pulled out a tattered envelope and more tattered letter written by his grandmother, Cathy, to his grandfather, Charles.

July 10, 2008....Dearest Charles: Tears fill my eyes today because I am afraid of what is happening in our country and to our civil liberties. Yesterday, the U.S. Senate passed a frightening bill (that is sure to be signed by President Bush) that gives sweeping powers to the federal government to eavesdrop, without warrant, on any citizen. Proponents say that there is nothing to fear unless you are part of Al-Qaeda, but you and I both know that giving such power to a president is another step toward governmental control and loss of freedom. **This day is a day that will live in infamy**.......*Always*.....*Cathy*

CHAPTER THIRTY-TWO
2084 – FEBRUARY 14, PM

Totally caught off guard by the aggressiveness and destruction ordered from The White House, newspapers across the country wrote parities on the Saint Valentine Day Massacre. But no one really knew what to do. The United States government had attacked its own citizens.

Michigan's governor was aghast, but her background as a television personality, didn't include an understanding of how or if the state should retaliate by calling out its own National Guard. Besides, since the Iraq war the National Guard had been taking orders from the Pentagon and the Guard had become a virtual acronym for the U.S. Army.

In fact, to avoid having the governor call out the Guard to protect the citizens of the state, the president had stationed platoons of U.S. Marines at each National Guard Armory to prevent entry by any state troops. When the governor learned of this tactic by the feds, she called in the head of the state police and the Detroit police chief, but neither had the weapons, material, nor firepower to combat the

Marines. The idea of war was anathema to anyone's thinking, but citizens had been attacked. The governor could not protect her citizens.

While the Marine and Blackwater-Xe killing exercise was over in a matter of hours, it was only the beginning of tedious, tortuous, unreal, unbelievable set of chaotic circumstances that had plunged the nation into some sort of war that had no name. It was not a civil war. It was the government attacking individuals. It was DC dictatorship, so Congress called itself into session leading to a 24-hour per day, round-the-clock, joint-session debate about democracy—where the majority rules—and—apparently—the majority wanted to see action against Muslims.

Opponents to the disaster cried: "What the hell has happened here?" One congressional pawn after another wailed without influence.

A report by the vice president to the Senate stipulated that the president had simply taken action against known or potential terrorists under the provisions of the Antiterrorist Act of 2083. This was the same legal maneuvering used by hawkish Republicans years before to validate the invasion of Iraq. The current veep told Congress: "We used the law to route-out potential terrorists that were on our own soil."

No one asked: *Is it right to kill potential terrorists*? [Years before no one had asked: *Is it right to torture potential terrorists*?]

Ohio's Senator Taft, a distant relative of former Senator Howard Taft, gained the floor by a unique maneuver called Rule of Personal Privilege, and he began a sort of unilateral, one-person filibuster under the Rule, which in reality was a speech, ranting and raving at his colleagues who abrogated their responsibilities in allowing one man—the president—to have enough power to declare war, this time on the nation's own population.

The nation was on the precipice of anarchy, and The Supreme Court had not even begun to consider the constitutionality of The Antiterrorist Act of 2083. This was an Act that the president was using at his personal discretion to initiate destruction and death to U.S. citizens.

Many times Chuck had dreamed the dream of this dangerous meeting of dream becoming reality. The Weismantels had been preparing for this day for three generations. The quiet underground concerns conceived by his grandfather and perfected by his late father were in place and now a militia, known only to a few, was about to be activated. Carefully under his control was an arsenal of defense. Soon a selected few would be called into action. The Detroit slaughter was not something that had not been anticipated. The defenders of freedom expected an attack just such as this. It was just a matter of where and when.

Chuck had been groomed for the occasion; even his choice of occupation and the first company that he worked for had carefully been selected to assure that an arsenal of armament would someday be at the disposal of selected modern-day minutemen. These patriots had been painstakingly planning how Americans would regain freedom when the federal government moved to totally control all of us, and to pointedly destroy those of us who didn't agree with those in power. Chuck had not known whether the move would be made by an out-of-control administration and president in Washington DC, or whether it would be a unilateral attack by a general — disgruntled or sane—who had control of an army. He now knew the decisions were coming from the oval office.

Detroit, however, came as a complete surprise to both Chuck and his cadre of supporters. All of their G-2 suggested that the region most apt to experience the unquestioned destruction of civilians was going to be in the West and carried out by either The Big Red One out of Kansas, or a group of fighter pilots based near Washington DC. Chuck also had no hint of Blackwater-Xe involvement. But, in a serious war analysis, Blackwater-Xe should have been suspect due to their Mexican border patrol assignment which placed them near Camp Pendelton, CA.

As daylight turned to dusk across the United States, everyone began to relive the experience of 9-11. Even though far fewer citizens were dead, the implications were actually worse.

During 9-11 all flights across the United States were cancelled except for a few special flights for Saudis approved by George W. Bush. Today's flights were cancelled, but for reasons of confusion and worries of a Muslim retaliation.

Every TV station in the U.S. carried 24-hour coverage of the event in Detroit....nothing else was news today. Soothsayers would forever suggest that this date, 2/14 was precisely selected to remind the Muslims that this was the same date that Israel was invaded, leading to the Seven-Day War. To suggest that this date was selected by the president only by chance would be hard to believe.

Chuck walked into the living room and just stood there motionless with his hands in his pockets. "Huh!" he said to himself because he felt a business card in his pocket, and, when he pulled it out, he read Gloria Switzer's phone number. He would not need that for awhile. Then, he starred at himself in the large **antique mirror** hanging over his fireplace—the one that had belonged to his grandparents. Perhaps they were trying to tell him something, for, why at this time, he asked........why did his memory recall an old cartoon that had been handed down to him from his grandfather? Clipped from the defunct Houston Chronicle, it was a comic strip by the name of POGO, and it said: "We have met the enemy and they are us."

omega

"Unrestrained government has proved to be a chief instrument in history thwarting individual liberty"

- BARRY GOLDWATER

WHITE PAPER:

The Hidden Cost & Pollution Aspects
of Solar Energy

By: Charles Weismantel
Kingwood, Texas USA

Recycling solar cells (arrays) is going to be a major financial and technological headache because environmentalists are not considering the heavy metal disposal thirty years from now.

Excitement bubbled as the homeowner of a new solar-powered house in Berkeley, California flipped the switch to the entry-hall lights as the family cheered their new home and its virtual electrical independence from the grid. Nestled on the hillside overlooking the University of California campus at Berkeley, the cost of this step-toward-energy-independence amounted to $30,000. But—this cost will be defrayed as a monthly fee paid to the city (amortized) over the thirty-year life of the home.....and.....the twenty-year life expectancy of the solar array. It all seems too good to be true.

And—it **_is_** too good to be true.

Neither the homeowner, the city, the United States Environmental Protection Agency (EPA), CARB (The California Air Resources Board) nor the garbage man has made one judgment about the chemical makeup of the photocells that make up the 2000 square foot panel that sits on top of the Berkeley abode. One can honestly say that there is no **disposal strategy** for the millions of solar cells that will be ready for the dump when they are no longer effective in creating electricity.

DANGERS OF SHORT TERM THINKING:

Both the EPA, and environmentalists in general, never ask the right questions when it comes to technology and when it comes to long-term effects of legislation that affects the technology. This is often because the government is run by attorneys who are not technologically savvy …and…because   many   environmental regulations are created by an EPA that is not savvy ... urged on by environmentalists who only look at part of what appears to be a solution—but—who certainly do not look at the long-term problems associated with the apparent solution. In the case of solar arrays, the most efficient conversion of sunlight to electrical energy normally is done by panels (hardware) that contains heavy metals—in particular selenium—and—it is important to remind the reader that selenium ranks right up there with lead and mercury as a pollution concern. It is a toxic heavy metal.

With the above in mind, let's review some real examples of short-term environmental thinking before tackling ***The Hidden Cost of Solar Energy***.

Computer and Flashlight Battery Recycling: For three decades individuals and companies have been buying new computers and associated hardware (routers, printers, scanners, memory etc. etc.) until one day someone finally asked two questions: (1) should we be putting all of this computer-related waste (and batteries) into a standard for-household garbage dump? And (2) Does this equipment have value that deserves to be recycled?

The answers—once waste engineers began to think about the problem—were obvious. Computers and associated hardware should <u>not</u> go into a garbage dump.....and.....yes... there is value in the circuit boards etc. etc. It makes sense that, rather than have to recover metals at mine mouth, there are metals in these components that are much easier to recover. For example—especially one can find advantages in recovering copper because copper ores, worldwide, and especially in the USA have become very lean. One should keep in mind that any heavy metals found in electronics (e.g. mercury amalgams or solders or chips and components that contain heavy metal) offer the potential of leaching (that metal) into the water table/water supply—particular if the garbage site is located in the *US Acid Rain Belt*. That belt can be defined geographically, mainly in the Midwest and Eastern USA, as land that is downwind form coal-fired power plants.

In light of this revelation (that recycling computers should have been considered from the start), one can begin to see a parallel with solar cells. But, there are other examples of very short-term thinking.

Gasoline Additives and Fuels: One of the most obvious examples is a US EPA edict in the 1980s that all gasoline must contain MTBE (Methyl Tertiary Butyl Ether). No one at the EPA stood up and spoke against the addition of this ether on the basis that it is toxic and is totally miscible with water. So, when traces of MTBE began to appear in pristine places (like Lake Tahoe) people finally began to ask questions that they should have asked up front (but did not). MTBE from leaking boat motors led to the discovery that this ether was also entering water supplies of Southern California. Eventually (after very expensive MTBE producing facilities were added at refineries) the chemical was forbidden.

One can also suggest that underwriting the production of ethanol from corn (as pushed and promoted by politicians from states that grow corn), has led to a price increase of food. The reader can be the judge of that consideration. But—as a companion example, the author has actual experience with the cost of producing biodiesel fuel. Financial Spread Sheets prove the non-profitability of this fuel when the feedstock-vegetable-oil costs more than $1.20 per gallon.

There is an additional political angle in respect to biodiesel fuel because the biodiesel-fuel specification, de facto, favors the use of soy oil over other vegetable oils. Again, this is, at least partially, a reaction to a strong soybean group lobbying in Washington DC. Any vegetable oil can be used to produce biodiesel fuel, in fact, the original diesel engines burn vegetable oil directly in the engine.

In the USA, algae (approximately 35% vegetable oil by weight) is an acceptable vegetable oil to make biodiesel fuel that would not compete with food oils. Ironically, an algae oil facility now operating in Nicaragua may find it more reasonable to use algal oil for cooking in lieu of importing vegetable oil.

The Hidden Hydrogen Story: If you ask most environmentalists this question: How do you make hydrogen? They will answer: From Water. That answer is wrong! The correct answer is: *Over 99% of the hydrogen in the world is made from fossil fuels—mainly natural gas (in a reaction called water-gas-shift).* Probably less than a half percent of the general public knows that hydrogen is made that way.

Given this fact, the winners in a hydrogen economy will be the refiners of the world (who now make most of the hydrogen anyway—to clean sulfur out of gasoline and diesel fuel). So—to make hydrogen, one processes a carbon-based fuel (with associated greenhouse gas effects and energy consumption) to manufacture hydrogen gas. Burning that gas is four times less efficient and less economic than burning the natural gas itself. Decades ago, these facts were presented to Congress in open session by the hydrogen guru of the world, Dr. Reuel Shinnar, City College of New York. The post script is that: *Dr. Shinnar also reported that making hydrogen from electricity (where electricity is provided by fossil fuel) is five times less efficient that using the water-gas-shift reaction.*

The conclusion is that—from a clean environment viewpoint—one must make hydrogen—not from water gas shift or fossil-fueled electricity—but from nuclear or from solar. By now the reader knows (or can review the literature) the pros and cons of nuclear power....and....now it is time to realize that **solar power is not a panacea**. It too has long-term and serious environmental effects and disposal costs (that are not considered by either politicians nor the promoters of solar power). If the bad environmental effects of solar power have been considered—the data and information is not widely publicized.

THE NEED FOR LONG-TERM SOLAR SOLUTION:

To begin with, one can suggest that (at least in the United States) the free market system should determine the winners and losers in solar energy. But—if that is the case—the players (the companies involved with solar power) should have a level playing field....and....that playing field should have an international flavor. For example, it is now suggested that some selenium-based solar cells are now the most efficient. (Personally, I do not believe there is enough selenium in the whole USA on which to base our country's solar industry....but...for talking purposes, let us say that selenium-based solar cells work ok, and there is enough selenium). Then—we have to ask:

How do you make selenium?

Are states going to allow (mining and processing and) discharges of selenium waste into our streams, rivers and estuaries?

Will the EPA pass regulations to ameliorate selenium regulations to benefit producers at the expense of the public? This happens with sulfur dioxide emissions. (See Box #1)

Are there air emission concerns? Remember......there is mercury in (as part of) coal and now the EPA is demanding that mercury emissions from stacks of coal-fired power plants (See Box #2) be controlled. Could we face similar situations in ambient air near selenium operations?

What if there is a selenium operation in the USA...which meets strict pollution control laws (air, water and solid waste)......yet..........a selenium operation in China can export that heavy metal to the USA much cheaper than the US manufacturer. Should we export the pollution problem to China in order to get a low price for the metal.....and....then we can establish rules for recovering the metal when the solar cells are spent....or.....do we send the non-working cells back to China?

Historically, these kinds of questions are similar to those that relate to casein (an ingredient that was widely used in Instant Breakfast). Both casein and powdered milk were given US government price supports at the same cents/pound. But—when milk was processed, the yield of casein (powder) was about half the yield (weight) as powdered milk....so.....all the producers quit making casein and made powdered milk (because the milk producers could get more money from the government by making powdered milk vs. making powdered casein). When the Instant Breakfast market took off, all the casein was being imported from New Zealand. When the milk producers asked for protection against low-cost imports, low and behold there was no one to protect because there were no casein producers left in the US.

The point is: *No one thinks these things through before the problems occur.*

Let me suggest to the reader that there ARE technologies available to reduce selenium in plant effluents. One such technology is to utilize zeolites (like natural clynotylite or artificial zeolites) to absorb and adsorb the heavy metals from the waste water. But—do you throw that heavy-metal-containing solid into a dump? If the dump is within the US Acid Rain Belt, the metal will leach out and get into the groundwater.

To do it right, the selenium should be recovered from the zeolite .... but .... that is going to take a process (perhaps electrowinning) that is very expensive. Ideally, heavy metals should be returned to the state of a non-leachable oxide.

The point is: *If you are going to be using solar panels that contain heavy metals, you better think things through from cradle to grave ...... and .... THEN compare the total real costs.*

Is the public aware of and willing to accept all of the consequences of solar energy—to include the fact that it is very possibly a large polluting technology? If the answer is yes, the public can vote to do so with their dollars. It would help tremendously if we could elect a few competent engineers as politicians who really could understand what is going on. It does not appear that we can always rely on the EPA because the agency has made a lot of mistakes— probably—in some cases forced or led by legislators and legislation that is less-than- good.

An alternative is to assure that we absolutely choose (and approve) solar technology that is totally environmental friendly. Movie actors suggest that one such solar collector (Detroit, MI) is made mainly out of inert plastic sheeting.......but........back of the envelope calculations indicate that using this technology in lieu of fueled power might require an area (footprint) as big as the state of New Mexico. And—there is another question: Is this technology efficient enough to make enough electricity to fit onto the roof of a person's house in order to supply the family's energy requirements?

The tradeoffs of solar energy must include environmental issues related to the manufacture of the cells themselves and the cost of their ultimate disposal. Solar technology's environment effects are still very much open to critique. Solar technology <u>has not</u> been properly questioned to include a cradle-to-grave scenario.

Unfortunately a lot of government money is at stake....and....big-company lobbyists are going to be knocking at Obama's door trying to get their share of the pie. Little companies, with unique technology (like SolarTech, Venice CA) are finding it hard to compete with the giants. At these small companies, money to build the Beta Product has to be taken out of the kids' lunch money. It will be very interesting to see what happens. Unfortunately, chemical engineers like myself can't even get in to see my congressman to talk to him about these kinds of things. Apparently one needs to visit a congressman's office with a checkbook in hand.

There is one final irony of the tremendous push toward solar power. A look at the basic raw materials to make solar cells also identifies the need for certain rare-earth metals....metals that are not-at-all available form within the United States, but mainly from China. Consequently, the USA moves away from being partially dependant on oil form the Middle East only to become totally dependant on energy raw materials from China. That is what one can expect when lawyers run the government.

BOX # 1
Sulfur Dioxide (SO2)

The US Environmental Protection Agency (EPA) has rightfully begun to fine plants that make sulfuric acid when the plant is emitting large amounts of sulfur dioxide gas. There are emission standards for sulfur dioxide because it is unhealthy and can cause environmental problems. It turns out that each acid plant is different....and....somewhere in the agency's control procedures there is a cost benefit analysis (that is also affected by how a congressman or senator wishes to interface with EPA to help a company or constituent).

As a chemical engineer one can understand that older sulfuric acid plants could have a more difficult challenge in meeting sulfur dioxide emission requirements than newer plants. Also, there are various alternatives to reducing stack gas emission that range from adding catalyst beds to simply putting on a caustic scrubber to treat the exiting gas. The end result is that EPA does not treat all plants equally, and the decisions for pollution control become an effort

244

of the agency's legal team + the agency's enforcement team. Best Available Control Technology (BACT), while desirable, is often not a factor in final emission requirements for a plant. The following table provides an example of recent emission requirements (set by EPA) for eight different sulfuric acid plants.

Plant Location	#SO2 per Ton of H2SO4	Total Tons Annual	Comment	Other
Texas	2.2	380	Refinery	
Louisiana	2.0	25	Refinery	
Oklahoma	1.7	92.4	--	
Wyoming	1.9	35	Chemical Plant	
Wyoming	2.1	38	Chemical Plant	
Oregon	2.4 Long Term	--	--	3.5 Short Term
Oregon	2.5 Long Term	--	--	3.5 Short Term
Ohio	1.9 Long Term	--	--	3.0 Short Term

BOX #2
Mercury (Hg) in Coal Stack Emissions

The US Environmental Protection Agency (EPA) has gone to great lengths to establish leachate tests for waste sites. Water moving downward through a pit, a dump or a toxic waste disposal site can be (or can become) acid in nature (that is, have a pH below 7.0). As such, this dilute acid can dissolve such things as heavy metals and carry them into groundwater. The idea of the leachate test is to reduce or assure that such movement is minimized. Standards are set so there is a minimal (or acceptable) amount of pollutants that leave the site and enter groundwater or tributaries nearby.

In the case of the metal, mercury (Hg), there is a move to collect this metal from stack gas from coal-fired power plants, using Activated Carbon (AC). The Hg, either as pure metal or as a mercury salt, collects on the AC and does not reach the atmosphere. The problem is: both mercury metal and mercury salts (that are collected on the AC) <u>do</u> dissolve in acid.

Consequently, when the AC is disposed of in the ground as waste, both the metal and/or the salt is leachable. There is the possibility of Hg (a poison) reaching groundwater.

One could pass the mercury-and-mercury-salt-containing AC through a Super Critical Water Oxidation (SCWO) reactor, and two things would happen. First, the carbon would burn and the heat could be used to create electricity. Second, both mercury metal and mercury salts would be oxidized to mercury oxide—and—the oxides of mercury are not leachable (and thus groundwater would be protected).

If a reader suggests that SCWO operates at very high temperature (above 1400 F, which is the formation temperature for Nitrogen Oxides [NOX]), the reader would be correct. There would be a tradeoff of having NOX enter the ambient air or having Hg enter the water supply.

The ultimate point is: *The EPA did not thoroughly think through the mercury disposal problem (or EPA accepted a less-than-perfect solution)… and … this is the kind of issue that we are going to face in the future when it comes to selenium (if selenium continues to be an acceptable material for use in the manufacture of solar cells.)*

PS: Photosynthesis is a most efficient use
of sunlight……
and
………..carbon dioxide is our nation's
second greatest asset.

FREQUENT FLYER BOOKS & MUSIC
(FFB&M)
PO BOX # 6713
Kingwood, Texas USA 77325-6713
PHONE: 281.358.6308

Additional books and music from FFB&M:
NEXT:

1.   Nelson   Gregory's   *"HARGRAVES of Homeland Security"* A hilarious but serious venture into how the USA is dealing with espionage and terror.......with romance as part of the mix.

2. *"HARGRAVES' Love Letters to JJ"* Nelson Gregory   provides   the   reader   with correspondence by HARGRAVES to JJ that rival the letters of Sigmund Freud to Meleva Maric`, Freud's first wife.

COMING SOON:

3. *"What Drucker Doesn't Tell You"* A how-to business book for managing the growth of a privately-owned business.

4. *"Policies and Procedures for Acquisitions and Mergers"* A series of check lists and questions to make sure a company does not get into

trouble when it buys or sells a business during the current economic crisis.

CHILDREN'S BOOKS:

5. "*The Green Duck, the Long-Nosed Pig and the Short-Necked Giraffe*" A read-out-loud book that proves how a handicap can help you become a hero. [100% of the profits from this book are donated to organizations that help children or adults who have birth defects or are handicapped later in life.]

6. "*e-mail Christmas*" A CD that will brighten your Christmas, make you laugh, and leave you singing.

Is this what Cathy meant (in Chapter 24)
when she referred to Islam as:

Islam: The Un-religion

When the average American thinks about
Islam, there are many concerns, and one can
point out that the most important thing which
favors the Muslims' efforts to establish a global
caliphate (and along the way, to exterminate
the Christians and the Jews or reduce them to
dhimmitude, which is the status of non-Muslim
minorities under Islamic rule), is the West's
casual, ignorant and stupid practice of viewing
Islam as a religion. Islam is *not* a religion; It is,
and has been from its earliest days, a
combination of religious woo-woo and a
totalitarian political system – inseparable and
inextricably mixed – with each promoting and
reinforcing the other.

To call Islam a religion is like calling a mule a
horse, or like referring to a serving of café au
lait as a cup of milk. A mule displays a
combination of properties – some derived from
a horse, others from a donkey – and – the fact
that a mule isn't a horse is utterly obvious. Only
willful ignoramuses will deny it. For as long as
people continue pretending not to see that
totalitarianism thoroughly pervades all of Islam,
just as donkey DNA thoroughly pervades the
genome of a mule, The Unites States will
continue to promote its own destruction. The
same is true for Europe.

Anonymous

DANGEROOUS TRENDS

OF

THE U.S. FEDERAL GOVERNMENT

Bill Nutz once said: "Whoever is in the saddle rides the horse to death." At the time, he was referring to either unions or to management, but the same adage can apply to politics in respect to Democrats vs Republicans or conservatives vs liberals. One can also suggest that Nutz' comment can be used in respect to the power of the United States Federal Government (or any government for that matter). The danger, of course, is that the more power that the people give to a president or to Congress, the less freedom they have as individuals, and one must be extremely careful not to give away freedoms as guaranteed by the Constitution and the Bill of Rights.

For sure, currently, there are national moves and pressures to take away the rights to bear arms. One can also see trends toward controlling the press (See *Language Police*) ....and .... In the case of the Iraq war anyone can review how Congress abrogated its right to declare war by giving that responsibility to President. Bush. One can see a trend toward abrogation, and lack of decision-making in both the House of Representatives and the Senate, in the way that these bodies have allowed EXECUTIVE ORDERS to take the place of legislation. In the process, secret happenings have been taking place under guidance of a GOP president and his peers leading to torture, illegal communication monitoring, and other unconstitutional action....not to mention the control that lobbyists have over all branches of government.....and now .. uncontrollable spending exacerbated by Obama policies.

The time has come to react to these problems and to attacks against freedom.

Nelson Gregory strongly urges the reader to review the writings of our Ninth President

William Henry Harrison

Two of his quotes are:

- There is nothing more corrupting, nothing more destructive of the noblest and finest feelings of our nature than the exercise of unlimited power.
- I contend that the strongest of all governments is that which is most free.

Made in the USA
Charleston, SC
18 December 2009